TIME HUNTER

THE SEVERED MAN

t-736

TIME HUNTER

THE SEVERED MAN
by GEORGE MANN

TELOS
.CO.UK

First published in England in 2004 by Telos Publishing Ltd
61 Elgar Avenue, Tolworth, Surrey, KT5 9JP, England - www.telos.co.uk
Telos Publishing Ltd values feedback. Please e-mail us with any comments
you may have about this book to: feedback@telos.co.uk

ISBN: 1-903889-43-X (paperback)
The Severed Man © 2004 George Mann.
ISBN: 1-903889-44-8 (deluxe hardback)
The Severed Man © 2004 George Mann
Time Hunter format © 2003 Telos Publishing Ltd. Honoré Lechasseur and
Emily Blandish created by Daniel O'Mahony.
The moral rights of the author have been asserted.

Typeset by Arnold T. Blumberg
& ATB Publishing Inc. (www.atbpublishing.com)

Printed in India
Hardback edition bound in the UK by Antony Rowe Ltd

1 2 3 4 5 6 7 8 9 10 11 12 13 14 15

THE TIME HUNTER

Honoré Lechasseur and Emily Blandish … Honoré is a black American ex-GI, now living in London, 1950, working sometimes as a private detective, sometimes as a 'fixer', or spiv. Now life has a new purpose for him as he has discovered that he is a time-sensitive. In theory, this attribute, as well as affording him a low-level perception of the fabric of time itself, gives him the ability to sense the whole timeline of any person with whom he comes into contact. He just has to learn how to master it.

Emily is a strange young woman whom Honoré has taken under his wing. She is suffering from amnesia, and so knows little of her own background. She comes from a time in Earth's far future, one of a small minority of people known as time channellers, who have developed the ability to make jumps through time using mental powers so highly evolved that they could almost be mistaken for magic. They cannot do this alone, however. In order to achieve a time-jump, a time channeller must connect with a time-sensitive.

When Honoré and Emily connect, the adventures begin.

DEDICATION

To Mum, who read me Mr Men *books when I was small.*

PROLOGUE

Screams.

Like wretched, tortured, agonised yowls, they echo into the cold emptiness of the room.

A base, animal whimpering, a gurgle of pain.

A needle and a hot, flickering flame.

Light replacing darkness replacing light, as if someone is staring at car headlamps hurtling along a road, as if they're watching the flickering on a broken television set that's been tuned to a dead channel.

And blood.

Lots of blood.

A voice is there, too, somewhere beneath the agony, rasping a name. It is laughing at the history that is dissipating all around it, swirling away into nothingness as the darkness moves in to swallow everything.

In this room, here, there is only the present, a long and torturous second stretched out and maintained, aloof from time, as if the rest of the universe has suddenly ceased to exist.

No one can remember how they arrived, or how long they have actually been here. Only the pain and the darkness remain.

A figure rises from somewhere in this darkness, but the view of it is hazy, dream-like, as if seen from behind a veil. It stares with shining, glassy eyes at the looping time streams all around it, watching as they bubble away into the future and the past, watching as they alter, ever so slightly, as the screaming comes to an abrupt halt and the ebb and flow of another existence dissolve against the persistent flow of time, dashed into fragments of nothing as if they had never actually existed.

Another one cut free, another one released from time's ticking bonds.

The figure steps away, carefully laying its implements down on a surface nearby. It wipes its hands on a dirty smock, and then steps towards another figure, this one prone, on a bench a few feet away.

Presently the screaming starts all over again.

For the tiniest of moments, the first figure hesitates, as if unsure whether or not to carry on, as if the horror of its actions has finally begun to register behind its eyes. But then it picks up its tools once again and the blood begins to flow down its arms, pooling on the floor in large puddles of glossy red.

This time the pain is different. This time it is far more acute.

The figure continues to labour over its charge, sweat running down its heavily-creased brow. After all, there are many others waiting to be released from their shackles, and tonight, it has much, much work to do.

PART ONE: THE SEVERED MAN

RAPID MOVEMENTS OF THE EYE

The marketplace was deserted, ethereally quiet.

Honoré Lechasseur felt the tiny hairs on the back of his neck bristle against the cold, and shivered. Spitalfields was usually thronging with people, even at this late hour. Empty, it just felt wrong, somehow unnatural. He shifted his feet and blew into his cupped hands in an attempt to keep warm. The fog was thick and penetrating around him, stifling the radial glow of the street lamps.

On the opposite side of the road, the scorched remains of the old church stood sentry-like against the moonlight, casting shadows across the street in wide, sweeping arcs. Around it, the remnants of splintered gravestones erupted from the soft loam, describing a shattered smile of jagged, broken teeth.

The shadows would be a good place to hide.

Lechasseur glanced about, trying to catch sight of his prey.

He'd been tracking the boy across the capital for nearly three hours, only stopping to catch his breath in the stolen moments before rounding a bend, or waiting to step out of a doorway. Now, he was cursing himself for losing sight of the child.

He stepped out into the road, listening for any sign of movement. Nothing. The marketplace was absolutely deserted. He glanced in both directions, up and down the road. The fog was everywhere, dampening the air.

He'd have to start again in the morning.

He sighed and turned about, ready to start the long trek back towards his lodgings.

Damn boy!

Then, in the quietness, he heard the scuff of a heel from somewhere behind him. He span around, catching sight of the child ducking around a corner just a few feet away, his ragged scarf fluttering behind him as he ran. Lechasseur took off after him. His heart rattled in his chest, pounding blood around his body as his legs pumped at the hard cobbles. He lurched around the corner, sure that he was only minutes away from finally ensnaring his prey.

Then, as suddenly as if Hades itself had just erupted from the ground before him, the world was full of light.

Lechasseur skidded to a halt and shielded his eyes from the sudden glare. It was blinding; a brilliant, hot white that emanated from somewhere – or something – a little further down the road. Between his fingers, he tried to make out what it was.

And that was when he saw it, a figure emerging from the whiteness like an apparition, or a tiny, fragile angel.

The girl in the pink pyjamas.

He shrank away from the searing light, covering his face with his hands ...

'Emily ...'

... and felt a firm hand on his shoulder, felt the faint whisper of a voice in his ear.

'Can you see it Honoré? Can you see it now?'

The darkness consumed him once again, and he was lost in a swirling mist of fog and dreams.

'Emily ...?'

Lechasseur sat bolt upright on his bed, sweat running in trickling rivulets down the fold of his back. His hair was damp with stale perspiration. He glanced around the room to make sure he was still alone. Bare walls stared back at him, gloomy in the inky wash of the moonlight. He allowed himself to breathe.

The dreams had been worse over the last few days; a procession of stuttering, random images that, upon waking, had left him with a sharp feeling of disquiet. But the whispering voice was new; a rasping, disturbing wheeze in his ear. He had no idea what it could mean, or to whom the voice was supposed to belong. Someone from his past, from the War? That would certainly explain the sudden flash of light; a flashback to Normandy and the explosion that saw him invalided out of service. But what it had to do with Emily, he had no idea.

He tried to put it out of mind.

Lechasseur swung himself out of the bed and padded his way over to the small basin in the corner of the room. The porcelain was cold and hard against his clammy skin. He splashed some water over his face, shivering momentarily with the shock, and then buried his face in the soft, downy towel.

Outside, the sounds of the city were slowly coming to life. He brushed the curtain out of the way and peered out at the street below. It was still dark. His tired reflection stared back at him from the pane of glass like a taunt. He watched for a moment, until his face was obscured by the streaky wash of raindrops being dashed against the window by the wind.

In the morning, he would talk to Emily.

In the morning, he would forget all about the dream, just get on with the day ahead and try not to think about sleeping.

In the morning …

He sat down on the edge of the bed and tried to stave off the tiredness that was creeping through his body like the slow onset of a lethargy.

He had to do something about getting some sleep.

Three hours later, Lechasseur began the slow walk across town to meet Emily. She'd decided to get a room of her own and had found somewhere she liked after a week or so of searching. It was close to Spitalfields, the place where she had been found by a policeman, wandering with no name and no memory. It was just a shame it was so far from Honoré's own place. He'd decided not to use his bicycle, thinking that he could do with the walk, but the cold was biting into his fingers now, and he was starting to wish that he had at least brought along some gloves. He jammed his hands deep into the pockets of his leather trench coat and stepped up his pace. Around him, the city was a hive of activity. Delivery vans trundled down crowded streets, whilst market traders set up their stalls by the side of the road. It was early, but Lechasseur had been up for some time; he was not a man who kept normal hours and, unlike most people, even enjoyed the bustle of the morning. Today he was tired, weary right down to his bones, but the fresh air was starting to brush away the residual cobwebs from the restless night before, and he could feel his mood beginning to lift.

He was anxious to put an end to the bad dreams as soon as possible. He hadn't worked for over a week, and needed something to get his teeth into, to take his mind off his own personal distractions. After he'd met up with Emily, he'd pay a visit to one of his contacts over in the West End, see if there was word on any of the police cases he'd been keeping tabs on of late. It didn't hurt to stay abreast of what Scotland Yard were working on; and occasionally, when the police seemed to be dragging their heels, Honoré had found himself picking up the trail, seeing if he couldn't bring a new perspective to the situation. It had been known to pay off.

He passed by an office building where the desk clerks were already hard at work inside. The tapping of their typewriters could be heard through a crack in the window, like the chattering of so many animals locked in a small pen. He smiled. Not the life for him.

In many ways, London was still an enigma to Lechasseur. The rain-soaked streets were familiar enough, of course, as were the people – the instantly recognisable cross section of humanity that inhabited any city the world over – but it was the *city* itself that still left him perplexed. It was as if the roadmap was in constant flux, shifting about him as he slept, so that he could never work out exactly what had changed. Sometimes it was as simple as a post box being on the opposite side of the road to where he remembered it, or yet another identical row of houses springing up in a place where he had never seen them before; but mostly it was less explicit, more to do with a *feeling* than anything more substantial. The city changed along with his mood, and he was unsure if he would ever get used to it. He supposed it was partly due to the extensive rebuilding that was changing the face of the city in the aftermath of the Blitz, but as much to do with the passing of time, the onset of entropy – a symptom to which he seemed unusually sensitive. He guessed it must have something to do with his strange connection to Emily, and his affinity with time itself; he didn't just *see* the city changing around him, but on some level was aware of the actual *process*, the organic alteration of the landscape. Places changed, just like people – that had been one of the most important lessons he'd learned. And London was no exception to that rule.

Honoré stopped briefly by the window of a bakery store, taking in the fresh smell as they removed a tray of warm loaves from the oven, but hesitated from stepping inside when, in the reflection in the window, he caught sight of someone watching him from behind. He immediately tensed. He studied the face in the window for a moment. The man looked old, his grey beard hiding much of his face, but his eyes were bright buttons, watching Lechasseur's back with a burrowing intensity. His long, scrawny hair was a mess of matted grime and dirt. The rest was obscured by the dazzle of sunlight on glass.

Honoré turned, but the man was already across the other side of the street, looking the other way. Honoré watched him, trying to ascertain what was going on. The man looked like a tramp; his clothes were tattered and torn, and by the look of him, he had been sleeping rough, spending the nights huddled in an empty doorway or curled up on a street corner like so many other of the dispossessed who inhabited this city. His hair was a ragged brown mop, and he carried with him a small satchel that he had slung casually over one shoulder. He looked like every other tramp Lechasseur had seen on the streets of London since the days of the war – homeless and hungry.

He took a step forward into the road, but stopped when he noticed that the man was talking to himself, or sniggering under his breath. Lechasseur's curiosity was piqued. He could sense there was something wrong. The man was definitely mumbling something, quietly, into his cupped hands.

He looked more closely, tried to see the man in the deeper context to which he was becoming accustomed. Each person had a time-snake, a thread through history that stemmed from the moment of their birth to the time of their eventual death. Lechasseur was sensitive to this, and could see people's snakes like an aura, could read everything about them from the impressions they had made on time, space and history, the footprint they had made on the fabric of the universe.

There was something *not right* about this time-snake, however – it stretched out in three different directions, each one ending in a tattered ribbon, as if it had been cut free from its purchase in the future or the past. These grotesque appendages curled around the man like a nest of headless serpents, medusa-like, whipping through time as if severed from reality. In the midst of it all, he babbled to himself, seemingly unaware of what was going on around him. The man was adrift in time, out of context, and clearly out of his mind. There was something infinitely sad about him, yet Honoré also felt a spike of danger in his presence, as if greater things were at work that he did not understand. To see someone who had just been *lifted* out of his own timeline – it just felt wrong, and his stomach turned at the thought of it.

He turned away and started walking, unsure if he wanted to see any more. He could feel his nerves jangling, could sense the man's gaze boring holes into his back as he walked.

He glanced at his watch – he was going to be late for his meeting with Emily. He ducked out of the way of a postman who was struggling with a large parcel bound for one of the local stores, and then he heard the voice ringing loudly in his ears.

'Can you see it Honoré? Can you see it now?'

He stopped dead in his tracks.

There was no mistaking it – it was the voice from his dream. It had come from somewhere behind him. He looked around.

Nothing.

It had to be the tramp.

Lechasseur ran back the way he had walked, his eyes flicking from side to side, trying to spot the severed man. He found the bakery he had been standing outside just a minute before. The man was gone. He stepped out into the middle of the road, trying to work out which direction the stranger had taken, but it was no use. It was as if he had simply disappeared, as if he had simply been swallowed by the spot he'd been standing on. Honoré shook his head, a strange, creeping sensation spreading along his spine. The dream had been one thing, but things had suddenly got very strange indeed.

He didn't hesitate any further. He turned around and walked as quickly as he could towards the café where he knew that Emily would be waiting for him. After the morning he had had, he was in need of a strong coffee.

OF SAINTS AND MADMEN

The Steaming Pot was filled with a cacophony of riotous sounds and the rich, distinctive smell of coffee. People bustled each other out of the way, reaching for seats or trying to catch the attention of the waitress. The chatter of voices provided a constant background hum.

Lechasseur edged his way past a row of women who were sitting by the doorway, drinking tea. He caught snippets of their conversation as he stepped carefully around them.

'Our Tom gets back from Wales next week ...'

'Can I pop around for a cup of sugar this afternoon?'

'They're rebuilding the old church round by Saint Chad's Terrace, you know ...'

Lechasseur smiled. Londoners. Not so different from the people of New Orleans.

Emily was sitting at a small table near the back of the room. She was wearing a white blouse, and her long, chestnut hair was loose around her shoulders, like a spray of water. In her hands she held a mug of tea, which she was sipping at in small, delicate bursts. She caught him watching her and smiled, waving for him to join her. He made his way over.

'Hi.'

'Hello Emily.'

He pulled out a chair and took a seat opposite her. Emily looked up at him and smiled, her pretty face shining in the low light of the café. Honoré slipped his black trench coat onto the back of his chair, and rested his hat carefully on the edge of the table, moving the sugar bowl out of the way.

'We need to talk. I …'

'Hold on.' Emily interrupted him with a brief nod of her head. He turned around. The waitress was making a beeline for their table.

'Good morning, sir, what can I get for you?' She wielded her notepad like a weapon.

'Just a coffee, please. Black. No sugar. Emily?'

'I'm fine, thanks.' She curled her fingers around the mug of tea on the table in front of her. The waitress slipped away into the throng. Emily looked up at him.

'You were saying?'

Honoré glanced back at her, exasperated. 'Not here. Let's walk after we've finished our drinks.'

'Okay. I don't have to be anywhere today.' She tried to catch his eye, concern evident on her face. Honoré looked tired, his dark skin had a faintly ashen hue to it, and there were darker patches under his eyes. His brown eyes still sparkled, though, and his beard was as immaculately trimmed as always.

'Are you all right?'

'Yeah. Tired, that's all. I've not been sleeping too well.'

Emily's eyes took on a slightly haunted glaze. 'Well, that's something I'm a bit of an expert on. Where shall we walk? Down to the market?'

A shiver ran unbidden down Lechasseur's spine. 'No. I can think of a hundred places I'd rather be at the moment. Leave it to me.' He stroked his short beard, tugging the fine bristles around his chin.

Moments later, his coffee arrived. He sipped at it quietly, hoping that the strong brew would help to banish some of the tiredness in his limbs. Emily was the first to break the silence.

'So, how's Mrs Bag-of-Bones?' She smiled, pointedly. 'It's been a while since I've been over.'

'She's well. Keeping busy in the kitchen. I haven't seen much of her myself recently; been too tied up with other things.'

That was true. He usually enjoyed sitting in the kitchen with his landlady, drinking tea. But since the dreams had started a few days ago, he'd taken to locking himself in his room and avoiding contact. He knew he wasn't himself, and Emily, if anyone, would pick up on his mood. Particularly after the events of that morning.

Honoré downed the remains of his coffee, and placed his mug pointedly on the table. 'You ready?'

Emily pushed her half-empty mug towards him. 'Yes. Let's go.'

Honoré retrieved his coat and hat and sprinkled a few coins on the table to pay for the coffee. On his way out, he dipped the brim of his hat at the gaggle of ladies who were still gathered around the doorway in deep conversation.

Outside, the air was pregnant with the promise of rain. Lechasseur adjusted his hat and buttoned the front of his trench coat. Emily walked beside him, her head dipped against the harsh wind. She walked close to Lechasseur, using his bulk to shield herself from the elements.

'So. What's been on your mind?'

Honoré turned to her. 'Dreams. I've been having these terrible dreams ...'

'Go on.' Her smile was delicate, comforting.

'I'm chasing a young boy across the city. It's late, and he keeps evading me, ducking around corners, hiding in shadows. I follow him for about three or four hours. We get as far as the marketplace at Spitalfields, and the place is deserted, no-one around. At first I think I've lost track of the boy, but then I catch sight of him, fleeing around another corner. I race after him, but when I get round the corner, the whole place lights up.'

'What do you mean? How does it light up?'

'It's like a brilliant, blinding flash; a hot white light that fills my entire field of vision. The whole street is just *white*.' He indicated with his hands. 'That's when I see you.'

'Me? What am *I* doing there?'

'Just walking out of the light towards me, like they described in the newspapers, dressed in your pink pyjamas.' Honoré searched her face, trying to gauge her response. 'I don't know what to make of it.'

'That's it? Just walking out of the light? What happens next?' She was eager now, keen to find out more. Emily knew almost nothing about her own past. She had literally *appeared* in the marketplace a few months earlier, dressed in her nightclothes as if she had just been plucked, unwittingly, from her bed. She had no idea where she had come from, or what her life had been like before she was found wandering about the marketplace, lost. All she knew was that she was here, now, in London, and the only person in the whole world that she could trust was standing beside her, telling her about his dreams. She craved anything at all that might constitute a clue to her unknown past.

'That's all. That's where the dream ends.' Lechasseur hesitated, unsure whether or not to go on. 'Well, it did until last night. Last night was different. This time I felt a hand on my shoulder and a man whispering in my ear.'

Emily was whispering herself. 'What did he say?'

'He said, "Can you see it Honoré? Can you see it now?" Then everything went dark again, and I woke up in a cold sweat. It felt as if someone was trying to tell me something.'

Emily studied him with her bright, shining eyes. 'I don't know, Honoré. I wouldn't read too much into all this. It's probably nothing – just a bad dream. You need to try and get some more rest.'

He could tell she was thinking exactly the opposite.

They were walking towards Covent Garden now, and the wind was buffeting them fiercely from behind. Above them, the sky was a dirty-static colour, but the rain seemed to be holding off, waiting for some ominous moment in which to open up the heavens. People were scurrying around, darting to and fro in an attempt to avoid the bad weather.

Lechasseur turned back towards Emily. 'That's just it. Yesterday, I would have agreed with you. But after this morning ... I'm not so sure. I saw something on the way over to meet you that made me change my mind.'

Emily stopped walking, and Honoré drew up beside her.

'You're serious, aren't you? You think there's something going on.'

'Emily ...'

'What is it? You know you can tell me. After all we've been through together in the last few months ...'

'Okay, you're right. I ran into a tramp. At first he didn't look different from any other tramp you'd see on the streets; ragged and covered in filth. But there was something not quite right.'

'Go on.'

'At first I thought he was like you, because I couldn't see his time-snake. But then I realised what was wrong. He'd been severed, cut out of time. It was like he'd been lifted entirely out of his timeline. He just *existed*, right here in the present, with no future or past. His timeline had three damaged ends, all flickering around him like headless snakes. And when he saw me looking, he started sniggering to himself, laughing under his breath.'

Emily looked appalled. 'That's *horrible*.'

'There's more. As I turned away from him and started walking, I heard a voice call out behind me ...'

'"Can you see it Honoré? Can you see it now?"'

Lechasseur was quiet for a moment. When he spoke again, it was in a broken whisper. 'How did you know?'

'Call it woman's intuition. So, did you go back?'

Lechasseur looked dubious. 'I tried, but he had already disappeared. The thing is, I can't seem to get his laughing out of my head.'

'And this happened this morning, just before you came to meet me?'

'Yeah.'

Emily placed a hand on her hip, as if she was thinking. 'Looks like we've got a bit of a mystery on our hands.' A pause. 'You don't think you're in any immediate danger, do you, from this ... this severed man?' She looked concerned, but resolved, even a bit excited at the prospect of another adventure.

Honoré met her gaze, a little wary. 'I don't think so, no.'

'Right then. I think it's best if you go home and try to get some proper rest. We can meet again at my room later on tonight. And then, when you're feeling a bit better, we'll see if we can work out who – or what – it is that's stalking you.'

Honoré smiled. 'Emily ... I'm not sure if I want to get into this.'

'It doesn't look like we have a great deal of choice. Look, I'm going to head home now, give it a bit of thought. You get some sleep, and I'll catch up with you later tonight. Get round for about eight or nine and we can have some food.'

Lechasseur shrugged noncommittally.

Emily turned away and started walking in the other direction, the wind whipping her hair up around her face in a frenzy of fluttering ribbons. After a few feet, she stopped and turned back to him, a smile creasing her face with compassion.

'Honoré?'

'Yes.'

'Try not to have any more bad dreams.'

Lechasseur watched her recede into the distance, and then adjusted his hat again, trying to stop the wind from lifting it free from his head. Emily was right – he did need to get some sleep. But home just didn't feel safe for the time being, not until he had a better idea about what was going on.

He turned about and, after looking around to ensure no-one was watching him, made his way slowly in the direction of Mr Sun's toyshop.

The toyshop itself was actually a pile of broken rubble, a building splintered apart during the great bombing raids of the Blitz and not yet cleared up. It was in a small side street, and all but ignored by the planners. But between the heaps of demolished brickwork, there was a crack in the ground, a space just big enough to squeeze through, that led down a flight of stairs and into an old, underground basement that had somehow survived the impact of the bombs. A friend had shown it to him; a friend who knew how important it was to have a bolt hole, a personal retreat.[1]

Honoré stepped down into the ruined storeroom. The place was filled with a dank, dusty odour, and the cobwebbed and rotting toys on the walls described twisted dioramas in the dim light, like tortured carnival players strung up in a dirty cell. The plants that had crept in through the cracks in the ceiling added to the sense that the place was some sort of ancient, gothic wonderland, remaining somehow trapped outside time whilst the city metamorphosed around it. Quite fitting,

1 See *The Cabinet of Light.*

when he considered the nature of his friend. Honoré supposed that most people would find the place haunting; but there was something quiet here, the type of peacefulness that you just couldn't find in most places around the city. Mr Sun's toyshop was a place where time stood still, where the constant background fuzz of the universe couldn't reach, where Lechasseur could relax and be himself.

He stood for a moment, taking it all in. Perhaps one day the enigmatic Mr Sun would return to the site of his bombed-out shop, but for now, Lechasseur would use it as a quiet place to get some rest.

He knew there was a kettle in the other room, but he couldn't be bothered to make himself a drink. He found a seat and sat down, moving an old hand puppet out of the way as he did so. For a moment, he studied its scarred, pitted face, and then he jiggled it around in his fist, watching its head lolling from side to side with the motion of his wrist. He put it down on the dusty tabletop nearby.

What if I'm nothing but a puppet, waiting for someone to finish playing with me?

The thought didn't bear dwelling on.

Lechasseur folded his hands on his lap, and sat back, allowing his heavy eyelids to close, blotting out the remaining light.

When he came to, it was already starting to get dark outside. Lechasseur clambered to his feet, stretching his body after sleeping awkwardly in the chair for so long. He felt refreshed, more energised than he had in days. And thankfully his sleep had remained dreamless, passing without issue. He looked at his watch. It was nearly eight o'clock. Time to be off to find Emily.

Honoré took one last look around the ruined toyshop before climbing up carefully through the crack in the ground, cautious that anyone might see him. The air outside tasted fresh and humid, and he realised it had been raining whilst he slept. There were a few people passing by, but not enough that he might be noticed. He slipped out from amongst the piles of rubble and stepped deftly onto the street, breaking into a stride, as if he had been strolling that way for the last half hour.

Emily's room was a good walk from Covent Garden. While he

walked, Honoré tried to play things over again in his mind. The dream seemed like a distant memory, but the events of the morning had been all too real. How could a dream, something so ethereal and insubstantial, be turning into reality? What did it all mean, and was he being influenced by some other, unexplained force? He'd seen the future in his dreams before, but the events had never been like this, never been 'real' until they had actually happened. This time, the other people in the dream – and, it seemed, in reality too – all seemed to know a lot more about what was going on than he did. And what was the connection with Emily?

He could go on analysing it for hours. He'd get round to Emily's place, have some food, and then they'd forget all about it and everything would go back to normal. He was sure of it. Right up until the minute he rounded a corner and saw the young boy playing in the street, his grey scarf fluttering about his neck in the breeze.

Honoré stopped dead. The boy turned to meet his gaze. They watched each other for a moment, both perfectly still, and then Lechasseur spoke.

'Have you been waiting here for me?'

The boy didn't move. It was as if he was rooted to the spot, petrified, like a statue made of flesh and bones. His scared blue eyes were fixed on Lechasseur, and his hands were clasped together, as if he had suddenly stopped clapping in the middle of a song. Lechasseur inched forward. 'What is it you want? If I can help ...?'

He stepped a fraction too close. The boy came to life. He bolted, flying off down the street like a startled deer. Honoré took flight after him.

The boy's time-snake whirled through the air, spreading around the child like a barrier. Lechasseur looked on as he ran, confused by the immensity of the boy's history. He had watched children before, been aware of the early stirrings of a new life, the very slight impressions they had made on the fabric of time, the untapped potential of their future. But this was something else entirely. The boy's history stretched right back through time, spanning human history like nothing Lechasseur had ever seen before. It was as if the boy was a conduit for time, a channel through which all human history flowed forth, yet also a passageway into the future. He could see nothing finite about this child's existence, only the impression that it had, and would, go on through time forever. It was utterly beautiful, yet terrifying to behold.

And one thing was sure: whatever he – it – was, it certainly wasn't the small boy it made itself out to be.

Honoré used a lamp post to help swing himself around a corner, feeling his lungs burning with the sharp intake of air. His legs pumped at the concrete, driving him forward, keeping the boy in his sights. He felt his hat lift from his head, but ignored it, figuring he could come back for it later. It was far more important he kept up with the boy.

The child wasn't stopping to look back. He wove his way down empty alleyways, flinging himself into the shadows, trying to make himself hard to see. Lechasseur rebounded painfully off a wall after sidestepping a spilt dustbin, but managed to stay on the child's tracks. Eerily, everything was happening in exactly the same way as it had in the dream. Honoré felt waves of *déjà-vu* as he ran, passing faces he recognised in the street, animals watching him from their garden perches, people's doors and windows opening and closing. He remembered, just in time, to jump to avoid a cat in the street, and realised that he hadn't even looked down to check if it was actually there. It was like he was replaying the whole sequence over again in his mind, only this time, he knew it was actually happening.

Too late, he realised they were heading towards Spitalfields and the deserted marketplace.

Honoré burst out of an alleyway into the main market square. The child was nowhere to be seen. He stopped for a moment to try and catch his breath, resting up against a nearby wall. He dragged at the air, rasping as he soaked his lungs with oxygen. The streetlamps nearby were emitting a pitched electrical hum. He looked around. A man was walking his dog over by the back of the old church, but otherwise the place was deserted. Honoré felt a shiver creeping down his spine. He'd seen this before.

He stepped out into the square, casting his eyes round in search of the child. Birds wheeled in the sky overhead, providing them a vantage point that Honoré would have paid dearly for. He called out, trying to break the sequence of what he remembered happening in the dream.

'Are you there? Come out; I only want to talk to you.'

His voice echoed emptily around the square.

He turned about, intent on leaving, on getting out of the situation before everything turned into chaos. He felt like he was being drawn into something dangerous, like he was acting out a predestined role that he had no way of altering or affecting.

Just like a puppet ...

Then he heard the scuff of the shoe from behind him. He turned about, slowly. The child was scampering around the corner, just like in his dream. He cursed himself for playing into the trap, but then went after him anyway, anxious to know what would happen next.

If Emily is around this corner, I'm going to ...

He rounded the corner.

Everything remained dark.

The child was tired now, and Lechasseur could see he was struggling to keep up the pace. He hesitated, standing at the bottom of the road, watching whilst the kid scrambled over the wall into the graveyard and disappeared from view.

So, no light.

That was an interesting, if unexpected, development.

He paced slowly up the road in the direction the boy had taken, and stopped by the wall, trying to catch sight of him. He was too late; the boy had gotten away. He scanned the overgrown tombstones in front of him, looking for any clues. He was going to have a hard time explaining this to Emily, when he eventually got round to her place.

He looked up. For a moment, he had the distinct impression that he was not alone. Was the boy still hovering around somewhere near? He scanned the area around him. In the distance, between the aged trees on the other side of the graveyard, he could just make out a figure, standing amongst the headstones, watching him. He looked more closely, straining to see in the dim light thrown down by the streetlamps and the silver sliver of the moon.

The tramp.

The tramp was there too, watching him. The severed man, with his broken time worm and bright, shining eyes. Lechasseur steeled himself. The man's severed history described concentric rings about his person, flickering as though electrically charged, warped images sliding past the nexus points at the end of each stump like a procession of random photographs. The man's entire place in time was hazy, indistinct. Yet somehow, it seemed as if part of his history was still alive, as if certain points in time were still active, still *inhabited* by this man. He had no idea what to make of it all.

They stood facing each other for a few moments, neither making any move towards the other. Then the tramp began laughing to himself again, a strange, sinister chuckle that left Lechasseur with a deep feeling of unease. It was too much. He leapt over the wall, shouting out to the man to stand his ground.

'What? What do you want?'

He pulled himself over the other side of the old stone wall, catching the hem of his trousers on a bramble bush and having to right himself before turning around.

As he'd anticipated, when he had righted himself, the severed man had once again disappeared from view.

He paced backwards and forwards for a moment, unsure what to do, and then clambered back over the wall, deciding it was time to fill Emily in on the details and attempt to find his hat. His hands and clothes were wet from scrambling over the dirty wall, and he needed a drink. The boy and the severed man would have to wait until the morning.

'So, you saw the boy, too!'

Emily sounded dismayed, but not, Honoré considered, for entirely the right reasons. He knew how desperately she needed to learn more about herself, about her own past – and her own nightmares – and the fact that she had been at home in the bath whilst he had been chasing the boy around London meant that another piece of her puzzle had just got thrown out with the trash. She wasn't about to do another magical reappearance in Spitalfields market.

Dreams, it seemed, couldn't predict everything.

Lechasseur had discarded his heavy coat and hat – which he had recovered from a puddle just a few feet from where he had lost it – and had taken a seat whilst she fetched him a coffee. Her voice echoed through from the other room.

'I've been thinking about our severed man. Why do you think it is that he's been following you around?'

Lechasseur studied the wall, trying to unravel the elaborate patterns on the wallpaper with his eyes.

'I'm not sure that he has been following me. It may be that we're both just interested in the same thing, whatever that might be. It could be that we keep bumping into each other by coincidence.'

Emily padded back into the room, her bare feet making little sound on the soft carpet. She handed him his drink, which he accepted gratefully. He allowed the hot mug to warm his hands.

'But what about the dream? He knew your name, and he knew about me. I think there's something deeper running through this that we still don't understand.'

Honoré was contemplative. 'You're right, of course, but I still can't see how we can look for any further explanation. I need to catch one of them to try and find out what's going on. The boy was almost the opposite of the tramp – too *much* going on in his timeline. But I think it's the tramp who's going to reveal the key to all this.'

Emily ran her hand through her hair. 'There is another way …'

He looked at her steadily, levelling his gaze. He knew exactly what she was referring to. 'Do you think that's such a good idea? Particularly since we know there's something wrong with his time-snake.'

Emily smiled, and sat down on the sofa opposite him, crossing her legs beneath her. She was wearing a pretty floral dress, and it fell about her as she sat, tumbling over the top of her knees and down to the floor.

Honoré sipped at his coffee.

'You said that he still had parts of it whipping around him, broken but still there. Is there no way we could try to jump to some time period that you can still see?'

He sighed. 'Actually, I saw more today when I caught him watching me in the graveyard. It looks as if there are three points of time that are still active, one at the end of each strand of his severed time worm. I don't know when they lead to, and I'm not sure that I really want to risk finding out. I mean, with a guy who's been cut off from his own timeline like that, how do we know that we're going to be able to get back?'

Emily shrugged. 'We don't. But we can probably rely on there being someone else around who would enable us to jump again. It might take us a few attempts, but I'm sure we'd get home.'

'I don't like it ...'

'You never do. But if we don't get to the bottom of this, you could end up chasing that boy around forever! Not to mention your lack of sleep.'

Honoré sat back in his chair, brooding. 'I'll think about it.'

He swilled the last of his coffee around in his mouth, and watched Emily as she collected his mug and paced back out to the kitchen. There was a brief clatter as she rinsed the crockery in the sink, then she popped her head back around the doorframe.

'Did you want something to eat?'

'Just something light. All that running around has made me hungry.'

'A sandwich? Cheese and ham?'

'Sounds great.'

She set to work in the kitchen. Honoré flopped back in his chair. He knew Emily was right about trying to jump around in time, but he just didn't want to admit it to himself. The idea of it made his flesh crawl. He'd be taking a huge risk; he had no idea what would happen when he tried to step into the timeline of a man who no longer existed within it himself. The repercussions could be horrendous. After all, the tramp wouldn't have severed *himself* from history, so there had to be someone else behind it. And that meant there was someone else out there with a lot more understanding of the time streams than Honoré Lechasseur. He scratched his leg absently as he thought it through. Not only that, but Emily had her own reasons for wanting to take another little trip.

Still, he couldn't see any other way.

When Emily came back into the room a few minutes later, he raised himself up in his seat. 'I think we should take a better look before we decide what to do. Scout around a bit, observe him for a while. You never know, we might find out what it is that links him with the boy?'

Emily put a hand on his shoulder, a gesture of complicity. 'We'll start looking for him first thing in the morning. Tonight, you can sleep on the sofa.'

Honoré was pensive. 'Oh, I don't think we're going to have to do much in the way of looking ... I think he'll be waiting for us to make the next move.' The last words were muffled as he bit into the sandwich that Emily had placed before him on the table, and he looked out of the window, using his hand to brush the curtains back from their frame.

Outside, darkness had engulfed the streets, and all he could see was the faint yellow glow of the city as its denizens retreated to their warm homesteads.

Somewhere out there, the severed man was waiting for him.

THE TRAMP

The morning came slowly, and when it did, Honoré was waiting for it, watching the sun rise through the drab grey curtain of clouds that had settled over London during the night. He'd sat for most of the night by the window, watching the world pass by. When he had slept, it had been fitfully, in short bursts, but thankfully there had been no reoccurrence of the previous night's bad dreams. Although that wasn't to say that he hadn't kept running it over and over in his mind, trying to work out what was going on.

He heard Emily stirring, and made his way into the kitchen, brewing them both some coffee. He made it strong, to prepare them for the long day ahead.

He was anticipating the worst.

An hour later, they headed out to Spitalfields market. The weather seemed to have broken, and the storms of the previous day had dissipated, leaving the air fresh and clear. Emily had nevertheless wrapped herself up in a large woollen overcoat. Lechasseur himself was attired in his customary black leather trench coat and hat. He was unsure how he was going to attract the attention of the severed man, but guessed that Spitalfields was the place to go. Everything seemed to centre on the marketplace and the old churchyard, and he hoped that if he waited there long enough, the severed man would come to him.

Emily was jumpy. She kept looking over her shoulder, as if she expected to see someone coming up behind them, taking her by surprise. Lechasseur did his best to reassure her, but he was feeling more than a little on edge himself. He scanned the road ahead of them, expecting at any time to see the grey scarf and black coat of the boy edging down the street towards them, or else the tattered rags of the lonely tramp who had found himself cut out of time.

They stopped to buy some breakfast rolls at a bakery they passed, enjoying the warm scent of the freshly baked bread, and sat on a wall nearby while they ate them. Emily asked him about his life as a 'fixer' before they had met, when he had made his living as a work-for-hire, often employed to track down a missing person or pass on some 'questionable' goods. These days, he walked a little closer to the line of the law, although he wasn't beyond using his own moral judgement when the police seemed unable to galvanise themselves to act.

He didn't tell Emily much, though, preferring to look forward to the future than to dwell on the past. Things had changed for him dramatically during the last few months, and he was still trying to unravel it all in his head. He was hopeful that, one day soon, he would wake up and suddenly everything would make sense.

He knew from his experiences in the War, however, that things were never actually that easy.

After they had finished eating, they walked the last few yards to the marketplace. The square was thriving with activity. Traders raised their voices to compete with one another over the abundant drone of the crowds.

'Oranges and pears. Get your oranges and pears here!'

'Stockings for the ladies!'

Emily led them through the press of people, winding her way between the stalls as they drew closer towards the churchyard. Lechasseur tried to take it all in, breathing deeply as they passed a stall selling herbs and spices from the Orient. The pungent aromas of another world filled his nostrils, the peculiar names on their little tags adding to the sense of the exotic.

Around him, children squabbled, pushing a ball backwards and forwards into each other's hands. He stepped around them as best he could, trying to avoid disrupting their game.

'Excuse me …'

Emily grabbed for his hand and pulled him forward, trying to hurry him on.

They entered the churchyard by the main entrance. Emily paused just inside, in the shade of a large tree, her face dappled with spots of sunlight.

'Where was it you saw him standing last night?'

Lechasseur pointed. 'Over there, between those two gravestones next to the trees. But I hardly think …'

Emily looked over to where he was pointing. 'It's all we've got to start with, Honoré. Let's just take a look.'

They wove their way through the maze of gravestones. Flowers, desiccated with time, poked their way out of little pots beside many of the overgrown graves. Honoré tried not to step on any of them as he clambered through the long grass. He came to rest beside Emily, who was leaning against one of the more elaborate gravestones he had pointed out from the gateway. His boots were damp from kicking his way through the long, wet grass.

'So now what?' he asked.

'I don't know. Perhaps we should split up, take a better look around?'

'No. I think we should wait. If we hang around here long enough, I'm sure that he'll turn up.' He stepped back, examining the weathered lettering on the headstone in front of him.

> Barnaby Tewkes.
> 1892.
> He Lives On.

The lettering was engraved on the slab in an elaborate gothic script typical of the Victorian period, with a number of garish embellishments such as cherubic heralds and religious icons. Very different from the graves that Lechasseur had helped to dig in the fields around Normandy during the War. He shuddered at the sudden, unbidden thought.

He looked up at Emily, who was screwing her face up in disapproval at the thought of waiting around for the tramp to show up.

'Look' she said. 'We'll make ourselves comfortable by that clump of trees. If he doesn't show up in a couple of hours, we'll head home and rethink the plan. There's no point searching the streets for hours on end, as we'll only miss him if we do.' Honoré edged around beside her, putting a hand on her shoulder.

'Besides. It's him who's been stalking me, remember. I've got no idea where to even start looking. I know it sounds strange, but something keeps drawing me back to this place, both in the dream, and in reality. It's like he's trying to tell me something. That is, unless you can think of anything better?'

She met his gaze. 'No, I don't think I can.'

'Right then, wait it is.' He used his foot to clear a patch in the mossy grass around the base of the tree, and lowered himself into a squat. 'Looks dry enough here. Come on.'

They sat in the shadows of the old sycamore tree, waiting. Behind them, the bombed out ruins of the old church loomed overhead like a scorched fragment of broken bone. They both sat in relative silence, neither of them having too much to say.

When Emily did finally speak, nearly an hour had passed, and she was clambering to her feet, wrapping her big coat around herself and pacing backwards and forwards in front of Lechasseur.

'I don't think we can wait around here any longer, Honoré; it's just too cold, and I think if he was going to show up, he would have done so by now.'

He looked up at her, nodded, and climbed to his feet beside her, a look of resignation on his face. 'I guess you're right. I think we're just going to have to wait for him to make the next move.' He put a hand on her shoulder to steady himself as he brushed himself down, flicking strands of damp grass from the back of his trench coat.

He felt Emily shift beneath his grip.

'Honoré …' Her voice sounded suddenly tremulous.

There was a rustle from over by the ruined church. He glanced up. The severed man was standing about ten feet away, his long hair flapping around his face as if he were standing at the centre of a tempest. Honoré had just enough time to notice once again the shimmering gleam in his eyes before he and Emily were swallowed in a brief electrical haze and everything disappeared from view.

PART TWO: MORS MORTIS REGINA

THE DARKNESS OF MEN

Night.

Enveloping darkness stifled Lechasseur like an oppressive blanket. He shook his head and tried to gather himself together. Complex webs of time described undulating patterns of complexity everywhere he looked.

He tried to focus. A bird, hopping down from a nearby railing, left a trail of spiralling depressions in the time streams, stretching out behind it like a wave. He could see how that bird would die, two months from now, choked to death in the thick smog of a London alleyway.

He clambered to his feet.

'Emily!' He steadied himself for a moment, trying to hold himself still. 'Are you there, Emily?' He could see barely more than three feet in front of him. The ground was cobbled underfoot. In the distance, he could hear the clopping sound of horses' hooves on hard stone.

He felt a hand on his shoulder, steadying him. 'I think we're still in London, Honoré. It's late. I can't see anyone else around.' Emily's breath made little funnels in the air between them. Lechasseur drew himself in against the cold.

'Victorian London, 1892. This smog is unbelievable.'

Emily looked up at him. 'How did you …?'

He shrugged.

'Never mind.' She hooked her arm through his. 'We'd better get ourselves somewhere warm. We can start looking for the severed man in the morning. What do you say?'

'Hold on …'

The sound of horses' hooves had grown louder, as if it was coming directly towards them. Lechasseur could now hear the creaking sound of carriage wheels being pulled along by the horses, rattling on the cobbled road. Dimly, through the thick smog, he could just make out the glow of a lamp, obviously hanging from the side of the carriage.

'Let's just see who we have here …'

Two horses' heads emerged from the soupy fog like phantasms, as if they had just been driven directly out of the netherworld. Honoré felt Emily shudder beside him. They jumped to one side as the carriage sped past, nearly bowling them over. The driver was stooped low over the reins, the curtains pulled shut so the mysterious inhabitants could not be observed. Dashed onto the side of the carriage in red paint was some sort of symbol, a circle with two points at its apex, reminding Honoré of nothing so much as a pair of horns. From what he could gather as the carriage flashed by, it seemed like a recent and hurried addition to the décor. At the sight of it, Emily emitted a startled gasp and fell backwards, landing awkwardly on the pavement by the side of the road.

Immediately, Honoré was by her side, scooping her up with the crook of his arm. She looked terrified, her eyes fluttering with nervous energy and her face was as pale as if she were a phantom herself. He held her for a moment, trying to ensure she had come to no harm. He wasn't sure what had caused her to react in such an extreme fashion, but didn't think now was the time to start bombarding her with questions. He guessed it must have had something to do with the symbol on the side of the carriage, and he closed his eyes for a moment, trying to commit it to memory.

He had no idea what it could mean. It was probably just a bit of graffiti that had pricked some latent memory, reminding her of something from her past. He propped her up, shivering, beside him, and together they watched the carriage trundle off into the distance, the diffuse glow of the lamp receding as it was swallowed by the murky fog.

After it had disappeared, and they were once again alone in the darkness, he turned towards Emily, offering her what he hoped was a reassuring smile. 'Come on. You're right: we should find somewhere to bed down for a few hours and wait until it's light. Tomorrow, we can start searching for the severed man, see if we can find out what's been going on. And besides, after that fright, you look as though you could do with a coffee.'

Emily nodded, shakily, and grabbed at the cuff of his coat, looking for something to hold on to. They turned together and began walking, one holding on to the other as they attempted to navigate their way through the dense yellow smog.

An hour later, they found themselves close to some sort of civilisation. The fog was still dense and obscuring, but tall buildings had begun to loom out at them from across the street, gaslights turned down low in the windows. Occasionally the chatter of people could be heard coming from a nearby side street, or else the sounds of yet another Hackney Cab trundling down a cobbled lane, the horses whinnying into the cold night air.

Honoré was a little dazed, unsure of his surroundings and edgy because of it. The fog gave everything a sinister edge, turning the once-familiar streets of London into a complex maze, where anyone could be waiting around the next corner, ready to pounce. He wondered, briefly, what had happened to the severed man.

Emily, on the other hand, seemed to be recovering well from her encounter with the mysterious carriage. She was acting far more like her usual self, and seemed quite at ease with their new surroundings.

'Let's see if we can find a boarding house where we can get a room for the night.' She smiled, leading the way down the street, but nevertheless staying close to Honoré for comfort. They ducked down a quiet alleyway and out into a large square. Houses ran around the edges of a small park, and a couple of people were moving about there, staggering into each other as if they had just been thrown out of a public house. They were both dressed in scruffy black coats and flat caps, and Honoré could smell the alcohol on their breaths even from across the street. He guessed they must be factory workers or local workmen. One of them turned and leered at Emily from the other side of the road, his mouth cracking open in a dirty, toothy grin.

Lechasseur turned protectively towards Emily, but his words were drowned out by the shrill, piercing scream of a whistle, sounding loudly in the alleyway behind them. They both span around at the same time.

Honoré was first to make a move. He darted back into the mouth of the alleyway, heading in the direction of the whistle. For a moment, Emily was left standing on her own in a whirl of syrupy fog, but then the thought of the two lingering drunks propelled her onwards and she went charging after Lechasseur, her heels clicking loudly on the bumpy, cobbled street as she ran.

Moments later, she came to rest beside Honoré, who was standing at the other end of the narrow passageway beside a uniformed man with a whistle in his hand. The man was tall and clean-shaven, and was wearing a large policeman's helmet with a shiny silver badge that read 'Metropolitan Police'. He was staring intently at something on the ground just by his feet. Lechasseur, catching his breath, was doing the same. Hesitating, Emily allowed her eyes to follow their gaze until they came to rest upon the object of their attention. She averted her eyes with a gasp.

A human body, sprawled out on the cobbles, its face all bloodied and raw.

She hadn't looked for long enough to see whether it had been a man or a woman. She wasn't even sure that anyone would still be able to tell. It looked as if some huge animal or beast had savaged the victim's face, tearing at it with demonic ferocity, its talons raking massive furrows across the flesh. She took a deep breath, trying to ignore the pervading stench of blood and iron in the air all around her.

There was something horribly familiar about the scene, and she shook her head, trying to shake off the alarming sense of *déjà-vu*.

The policeman seemed to be frozen in some sort of shock. Emily studied his face, as much to avoid looking at the body as for any other reason.

He looked cold and inexperienced, unsure what to do, and was staring down at the corpse as if he expected it to move, or to miraculously reveal to him what had happened. His whistle was hanging limply in his left hand. Emily realised that he must have been only about twenty years old.

Exasperated, Lechasseur knelt down to take a closer look at the body.

'He was thirty-five, a salesman, been drinking in the pub just down the road from here. *The ... ah ... The Tailor's Arms.*' He paused for a moment, contemplative, and then looked up at the police officer. 'It looks like he's been savaged by some sort of animal. What do you think? A rabid dog?'

Emily got the impression that a rabid dog was the last thing Honoré considered to be responsible for the state of the disfigured corpse in front of him.

The police officer, startled, looked at Lechasseur as if he'd only just realised that the other man was present. He shot Emily a nervous glance, then tucked his hand behind his back to pull out his truncheon. Lechasseur got to his feet. The officer took a step backwards, and then brandished his weapon.

'You seem to know an awful lot about the circumstances surrounding this suspicious death. Particularly for a, um, *foreigner*. Would you care to elaborate down at the station?'

Lechasseur stared at the man, barely containing his anger. He had expected the values of the Victorian Londoners to be outdated and hypocritical by his own standards, but this was something else. His fists clenched and then unclenched by his side. He turned to Emily.

'Come on, we're leaving.'

Emily gave him a small, suspicious nod. They linked arms and began walking back the way they had come.

Again, they were stopped by the piercing scream of the policeman's whistle.

'*Halt!* I am arresting you in connection with the violent death of this man. You may not leave the immediate vicinity until a police escort has arrived, at which point you will be escorted back to the station for further questioning. You will both be held until the superintendent is satisfied as to the question of your guilt.'

The boy held out his truncheon, shaking a little with nervous energy and adrenaline.

Lechasseur stopped and turned about to face the man in the uniform. He could hear footsteps now, other officers running towards the scene from a number of different directions, called away from their own duties by the urgency of their comrade's whistle. He hesitated for a moment, debating the possibility of fleeing. Emily was standing just behind him.

The constable shifted awkwardly, unsure how to react to the big American in front of him, dressed in a strange black cloak of leather, an oddly-shaped hat resting on top of his head. Lechasseur, in turn, tried to gauge the young man before him. He watched the man's history spiral out from him like a map of his past, a rich tapestry of his future. It bloomed all around him, telling the tale of his life. Honoré could see his difficult childhood in the slums, his mother forcing him to enrol in the police force, his first kiss with a girl. He could also see him being beaten with his own truncheon, a gang of thugs holding him down whilst they took it in turns to batter him, bludgeoning him into the ground in an alleyway not dissimilar to the one they were standing in now.

When he finally spoke, Lechasseur's voice was measured and calm. 'I can assure you that neither I nor my lady friend had anything to do with the death of this man. We came to your assistance when we heard the sound of your whistle from nearby. Besides, the man has been utterly savaged. If we had done that, don't you think we would have been covered in blood? Look at the marks around his throat.' He waved his hand to indicate. 'Not to mention the fact that his right hand is almost totally missing, where he must have tried to fend off the creature as it attacked him.'

The police officer looked him in the eye, unsure.

Lechasseur continued. 'The fact that the body is still steaming where the face has been torn open should give you some idea how fresh the attack must be – we walked down this alleyway just a few minutes beforehand and saw nothing of note.'

There was a commotion then, as a number of other policemen arrived at the scene almost simultaneously, each of them screwing his face up in disgust at the sight of the body lying spread out on the floor. They formed a loose semi-circle around it, taking in the stand-off between Lechasseur and the young constable.

Emily gave a gentle shudder beside Lechasseur as she glanced at the corpse again, watching the steam rising out of the warm body in little clouds, spiralling into the cold night air. The stench of blood was horrific.

One of the other officers, a man with a bushy moustache, glanced at Emily and Lechasseur and then looked back at the officer who had called them all to the scene.

'What's the story with these two?' He nodded in their direction. 'Anything to do with this?' He pointed at the body almost nonchalantly, as if it were a sack of potatoes or a butchered pig.

The constable looked back at him nervously. 'I'm not sure yet. I believe they should be taken in for questioning.' He lowered his truncheon a little as the other man appeared to take over.

Lechasseur stepped forward. 'Now, hold on a minute. My friend and I have absolutely nothing to do with this. We were out for a walk and looking for somewhere to stay the night when I heard the whistle and came running back up the alleyway here.'

'*Back* up the alleyway?'

'Yes, back up the alleyway. We'd walked this way just a few minutes before. We came across a couple of drunks in the square down there. You'll probably catch them if you send a man now.'

'So, you came *back* up the alleyway just after you heard the police whistle, minutes after a murder had occurred on this very spot, and the only evidence you have to say that you're not involved is the testimony of a couple of drunks? I should say you're in for a long night of questioning back at the station.'

The officer with the moustache took a step forward, a couple of the other men stepping in behind him. Lechasseur tensed.

Emily skipped around in front of him. 'Look, I can assure you we are only two honest civilians who came to assist when we heard the police whistle sound a few moments ago. Let's talk about this for a moment and I'm sure we can make our position clear.'

'Please step aside ma'am, this doesn't concern you.'

Emily remained steadfast.

The constable with the moustache drew closer.

'Ma'am, step out of the way. We don't want you getting hurt now, do we?'

Emily took a step backwards towards Honoré, who was already moving around her to confront the gathering circle of men.

'Look, I don't know what it is that you want from us but …'

Lechasseur was caught by a blow to the face mid-sentence, and dropped to the floor, clutching at his nose. Emily caught sight of the young constable backing away as the older men moved in, surrounding the big American. She moved to go to his aid but one of the other men blocked her way. There were six of them now, drawing in to circle Honoré completely, penning him in like he was some sort of temperamental animal in need of restraint.

Honoré clambered back to his feet and gathered himself together, his nose bloody from the impact. He wiped the back of his hand across his face, and stood, eying his opponent and refusing to take the bait and retaliate. He wasn't going to be the one to start an all-out fight, especially with these odds.

'Not from these parts are you? Like murdering good English folk do we? Is that where you get the money to buy fancy clothes like these? Eh?'

The sergeant jeered at Lechasseur, indicating his leather trench coat with a wave of his hand.

'Look, I've told you, I've got nothing to do with this dead man. Can't you see that he's been killed by some sort of animal?'

'I can see nothing of the sort. We're taking you to the station for questioning.' The man turned and stepped away, waving a hand at his colleagues as he did so.

Two of the others stepped in closer and started throwing punches at Lechasseur. He put his arms up to defend himself, trying to stave off the beating, but their fists rained down on him relentlessly, pummelling him to the ground.

Emily, screaming in protest, threw herself at the moustachioed sergeant, but he slapped her away and she fell to the floor awkwardly, scrabbling at the cobbles. At this, Honoré finally allowed his anger to take over and tried desperately to fight back, even managing to land a few retaliatory blows on a couple of the men, but there were simply too many of them, and he was soon overwhelmed.

When they finally stepped back from him to catch their breaths, he was curled up in a heap on the ground, bloodied, battered and bruised.

Emily, alone and frightened, sat down beside him on the cobbles, tears streaming down her cheeks.

Just a few feet away, the dead man watched on in silent, eerie vigil, his unmoving eyes seemingly taking in all that was happening nearby.

THE HANGED MAN

When Lechasseur finally regained his senses, he was lying on a hard bed in a small, dark cell, somewhere on the other side of the city. He had a vague recollection of being dragged into a police carriage along with Emily and being towed to the station, but he guessed he must have slipped in and out of consciousness during the short journey, as his memories were all fragmented and made little sense.

He sat up on the bed, cringing at the smarting pain in his side. His head throbbed with an agonising rhythm. He ran his hands gently over his face, feeling where the welts had appeared in the time since his beating in the alleyway. Dry blood was encrusted in his beard and his lip was swollen where it had split open during the fight. It must have been a few hours.

He felt around, looking for a way to get a drink of water.

Then he stopped, sensing for the first time since waking that he wasn't alone. There was someone else in the cell.

'Emily? Is that you, Emily? Are you okay?'

A harsh, rasping laugh came from the shadows at other side of the little room. Honoré could see no more than a few feet in front of his face.

'Sorry matey, no such luck. I ain't no lady friend of yours.'

The man's face appeared out of the gloom, and Honoré felt the hairs on the back of his neck prickle with caution. The man was a giant, rising a good seven feet off the ground, with a rough, shaven head and stark, staring eyes. He shambled over towards Lechasseur and handed him a bowl of water.

'Looks like you took a bit of a beating last night.' It was a statement rather than a question, and Honoré nodded silently in reply. The pain in his side was excruciating.

He took a swig from the bowl of water, trying hard not to notice it was tepid and tasted like it was three days old. He handed it back to the other man when he was done.

'Thanks.'

'No problem. So, what did you do to end up so badly beat on?' The man's voice was a low growl, a gravely, grating rasp that Honoré guessed must have had something to do with the lurid purple scar that curled around his throat like a pair of neatly pursed lips.

Honoré was pensive, not wanting to give too much away. 'Someone took a dislike to me because I wasn't from around these parts.'

'Aye. A familiar story.' The man broke into a wheezing cough, emitting a kind of strangled gargle, before righting himself and spitting, loudly, on the floor nearby. He looked at Lechasseur expectantly.

Honoré decided it would be better not to ask.

'They tried to hang me for something I didn't do. Bastards.' He spat on the floor again. 'Accused me of being involved with that cult, the missing girls and murdered whores. The girl they tried to hang me for, they couldn't even find her body. Still, can't keep Horace McEaseby down for long, eh?' He chuckled, more to himself than to Lechasseur, who shifted a little on the bed, wary of what McEaseby might do next.

The big man smiled. 'So, you'll be anxious to know what happened to your lady friend, then?'

Honoré looked him straight in the eye. 'You know what happened to Emily?'

'I saw what they did to her after they pushed you in here.'

Lechasseur was on his feet. 'And ...'

'And they stuck her in the cell next door. They may be bastards, but they ain't stupid. They wouldn't touch a lady dressed like that. At least, not until they've found out who she is.'

Honoré sat down again, relief washing over him. At least Emily was safe. Now all he had to do was work out how to extricate them both from their current, unhappy situation.

'How long have you been in here?'

McEaseby smiled. 'Too long. I can't count, but I've been scratching the wall every morning.' He indicated with his hand, and when Honoré looked, he was shocked by the number of tiny lines that McEaseby had scratched into the stone wall by his bed. 'I was here all through the winter months. Nearly froze to death. It's not so bad now the cold has broken; at least I get a warm meal from time to time.'

McEaseby took a draught from the bowl of water in his hands, before placing it back on the floor by his feet.

Honoré studied his face. 'Do you think they'll try to hang you again?' He shivered at the thought.

'Who knows? But they couldn't finish me off last time, so I'll keep fighting them 'til the end.' McEaseby chuckled, a harsh, half-strangled sound that made Lechasseur bristle in sympathy and disgust. He was avoiding looking at McEaseby for too long in case he accidentally saw something he didn't want to; this was one man he could imagine coming to a sticky end, and Honoré didn't want to have to face him again, knowing how he was going to die.

Instead, he stood up.

'I'm going to see if Emily's okay ...'

He tottered for a moment before righting himself and padding over to the bars at the front of the cell. For the first time, it occurred to him that he was missing his hat. He must have lost it in the brawl in the alleyway. He pushed himself up against the bars and raised his voice a little.

'Emily? Are you there?'

There was no reply.

'Emily? Are you awake?'

'I'm here, Honoré.' It was a faint reply, stifled by the oppressive atmosphere of the underground holding rooms. There was a shuffling sound as she made her way to the front of her own cell. 'Are you okay?'

'A little bruised and sore. Nothing a good bath and some sleep wouldn't sort out. How about you? I saw one of them push you over in the alleyway. Are you hurt?'

'No, I just grazed my knee. My dress is torn to shreds, but that's nothing we can't fix either.' She sounded relieved, if a little tired.

Lechasseur smiled.

'Honoré?'

'Yes?'

'What do you think is going to happen next?'

McEaseby chuckled to himself loudly in the background.

'I've got no idea. But my guess is we're going to be questioned about last night.'

'So what are we going to say? That we came here from the future looking for a man who's been cut out of history? We'll be inside a padded cell by the end of the day.'

The laughing behind Honoré stopped short.

'Then keep your voice down!' he hissed. 'I'm working on it. Sit down and try to get some rest. I'll shout for you if I have any other ideas.'

Lechasseur, shaking his head, turned away from the bars and retreated slowly into the gloom at the back of the cell. He caught sight of McEaseby watching him from his bed, his eyes gleaming in the murky light. Lechasseur remained expressionless, and, soon enough, McEaseby glanced away. But Honoré could feel the scrutiny in that gaze, could sense that something inside the cell had changed after his conversation with Emily. He wondered what McEaseby had heard that had made him clam up so completely.

Shuddering, he resolved to stay awake until someone came to get him from his bed.

A KIND OF JUSTICE

After about an hour, the silent monotony was disturbed by the clinking of a key chain and the sound of two men coming through the iron gate that led down into the underground lockup where Emily and Lechasseur were being held.

Honoré stood as the men approached the entrance to his cell. McEaseby stirred, but didn't get up from his bed.

After a moment, a man in uniform noisily unlocked the cell door, and the two newcomers stepped inside. The constable was carrying an oil lamp and, after fumbling for a minute, he unsheathed it, partially lifting the metal shutters around the edges to release the light into the room like a soft cascade of liquid gold.

Honoré felt his eyes recoil from the sudden glow, and had to fight to try and make out what was going on. McEaseby shifted around on his bunk, burying his face in the crook of his elbow.

'This is the man, sir; found him hanging around the body we did, like a vulture or something.' The man's voice was nasal, weasely.

'Yes, that will be all, Stokes.' The other man, who was dressed in a pale brown suit and tie and had a small bowler hat perched on top of his head, cleared his throat and looked straight at Honoré. 'Sir, may I beg of you your name?'

Lechasseur looked back at the man quizzically.

There was a brief pause.

'Oh, I do apologise. The name's Newman, Sir Charles Newman, New Scotland Yard.' He stepped forward, proffering his hand.

For a moment, dumbstruck, Lechasseur didn't react, but then he reached out and took the man's hand, shaking it firmly.

'Honoré Lechasseur.' His eyes were still smarting from the light. Nevertheless, he managed a brief appraisal of the man in front of him. He was certainly not the sort of man he would usually associate with the police; he looked uncomfortable standing there in the cell. But something told Honoré that there was much more to Newman than was immediately apparent. He had the air of someone foppish and well-to-do, but Lechasseur could see beyond that to the cool intellectual hiding beneath, and knew he would be foolish to dismiss him; Newman had seen things, and, like Honoré himself, he knew the world.

Honoré steeled himself and looked the other man in the eye. 'I believe there's been a case of mistaken identity. Your officers seem to have taken me for a dog.' He let that hang.

Newman looked pained. 'Indeed.' He paced a couple of times in front of Lechasseur. 'I think it best we take a short trip back to the Yard. We can collect your lady friend on the way.'

Honoré smiled. At last, things seemed to be going a little more his way.

'I believe Emily is in the next cell.' He waved his hand, and Stokes, after a nod from his superior, disappeared to go and fetch her.

'Ah, yes, Emily is it? I do apologise for the rather discourteous manner in which you've both been treated.'

Honoré rubbed his bruised face in reply. 'Hmmm.'

'I have a bottle of brandy back at the Yard. I'm sure you could do with a stiff drink and an opportunity to wash.'

There was a moment of silence as both men waited for Stokes to return with Emily. McEaseby snorted to himself from the other side of the room.

After a minute or two, there was a shuffle of feet from outside of the cell, and Newman beckoned to Lechasseur, indicating that he should step out into the passageway.

Emily was waiting outside, with Stokes standing behind her, a look of disgust evident on his face. When she saw Honoré emerge from the gloom, she gasped in shock.

'Oh Honoré, your face …'

Lechasseur smiled at her. 'Don't worry, most of it will wash away … I've been through worse.' At that, Stokes raised an eyebrow at his superior.

'Yes, well, let's see what we can do to get you all cleaned up. Stokes,' he looked at the other man pointedly, 'have a carriage brought around to the front of the station, post-haste.' Stokes shuffled for a moment from foot to foot.

'Well, don't keep me waiting, man.'

The small, shrew-like character scuttled away into the gloom.

Emily moved closer to Lechasseur and put a hand on his arm. 'Are you really okay, Honoré? You look hurt.'

'Just a few bruises. Nothing I can't handle. The sooner we get out of here, the better, as far as I'm concerned.'

Emily nodded in agreement. 'And then we need to talk. I've been thinking all night about that severed man. I've got a few ideas …'

Honoré stopped her mid-sentence with a gesture of his hand. 'Not now. Later.' He nodded at Newman, who was waiting for them at a polite distance. 'Let's find out what we can here before we make any more plans.'

'But …'

'Come on, we're off to New Scotland Yard.'

They caught up with Newman and skipped up the short flight of steps towards the main part of the police building. Newman held the door open for them as they passed through.

A number of the constables who had beaten Lechasseur the previous evening were sitting around a table behind the main desk, playing cards. Newman cast his eye over them.

'Quiet day, lads?' It was obvious from his tone that he was far from impressed.

One of the men looked up, the contempt clearly evident in the set of his jaw. When he saw Lechasseur standing beside Newman, he sneered. 'Off to the Yard are you? Saving us the bother of questioning him, eh, boss?' The others sniggered. Newman stood for a moment, glaring at him, barely containing his anger. His face flushed. Then he turned around and marched out of the door, his back to the laughter of the other men.

Emily and Lechasseur followed close behind him.

Outside, their carriage was waiting. The morning sun was bright in their eyes after the darkness of the holding cells, and both Emily and Honoré had to shield their faces as they clambered up into their seats.

Presently, the snap of a whip indicated they were on their way, and the two of them sat back, exhausted.

Newman, sitting opposite, didn't speak for the entire time it took to make their way across the city to New Scotland Yard.

The building was a massive, imposing structure that sat on the bank of the Thames, overlooking the sprawling metropolis of the Victorian capital. Emily, climbing down from the carriage, took in the view with some surprise.

'Honoré, it looks … different, somehow. More grand, more stately.'

Newman smiled at her with a look of pride, misunderstanding her comment as a comparison with the original Scotland Yard, from which the Metropolitan Police had moved some two years earlier, in 1890.

'It's magnificent, isn't it?, Fifteen thousand men operate from inside this building, working day and night to keep the city safe from criminals and madmen.'

Lechasseur smiled at Emily, wincing momentarily as his bruised face cracked with the movement. He knew as much as anyone about the changing face of the city. 'Come on. Let's go and get cleaned up.'

They followed Newman slowly inside.

After they had both been given the opportunity to wash and freshen themselves up, Newman guided them through a maze of corridors to his small office on the building's second floor, pausing only to collect a plain manila file from one of his colleagues. His room smelled somewhat stale, like it was rarely used but cleaned regularly, so that the bleach and soap had worked their way into the surfaces, giving the place an atmosphere that reminded Honoré of the inside of a hospital. He wrinkled his nose as they stepped inside.

Newman bade them take a seat, while he shuffled around in a filing cabinet behind his large, impressive desk then produced a small bottle of brandy with a flourish and a smile. He made his way over to a small sideboard beside the window, where he rooted out three mugs and poured each of them a measure of the strong liquor.

As he handed them their drinks, apologising for the lack of glasses, Emily stood and took in the view from the window, looking out over the river below as it stretched away, snaking its way through the city like a long and muddy snake. People stood on a platform by the edge of the water, waiting to take a ride in the boats that shunted their way up and down the waterway throughout the course of the day.

Honoré watched her for a moment. The sunlight was dappling her face, and her petite form was now wrapped in a long, elegant Victorian dress that Newman had arranged for one of the maids to provide whilst they washed. He wondered, for a brief moment, what it was about this young lady that had caused their lives to become so entangled, that had sparked such a bizarre symbiotic relationship, which, somehow, had caused them to end up in the office of a Scotland Yard detective in the middle of Victorian London. He almost shook his head in disbelief.

He turned to Newman. 'So, why are we here?'

The other man looked a little startled at the abruptness of the question.

'Well, it's, erm …'

Emily turned away from the window to watch them both, her fingers curled around the sides of her mug. She took a small sip of her brandy, and shivered as it spread tickling fingers of warmth down throughout her body.

'The thing is … there's been another murder.'

Honoré seemed suddenly to snap to attention. 'When?'

'Whilst you were already in custody. Last night.' Newman opened the file that had been handed to him by his colleague, and consulted the notes therein. 'The second victim, a man in his fifties, was found dead at around three o'clock this morning, killed in an almost identical manner to the unfortunate chap that you happened upon last night.'

Lechasseur looked evenly at Newman. 'So, when we're done here, we're free to go? I presume you won't be intending to question us further after this second incident?'

Newman smiled, softly, although Emily could see that he was feeling a little tired and strained. 'Quite.' A pause. 'Although I would appreciate it if you could enlighten me a little as to the circumstances that led up to your rather ... sorry encounter with the officers last night. May help with the investigation, you see.' He stroked his neat moustache as he spoke, and when he had finished, picked up his mug of brandy and helped himself to a brief, stiff drink.

Emily looked at Honoré, who seemed to have glazed over and was staring into the middle distance, somewhere just over Newman's shoulder. Hurriedly, she tried to catch Newman's attention.

'Of course, Inspector, we'll do whatever we can to help.' She paced across the room and took a seat beside Lechasseur, placing her drink on the edge of the desk before her. She looked at Newman, nodding for him to continue.

He did so, hesitantly. 'Recently, the killer seems to have increased the frequency of his attacks. There have been twelve in total, all in different areas of the city, all without witnesses or any substantial form of evidence. The trail was absolutely cold. That is, until the two of you came along.' He looked over at Lechasseur, who blinked, suddenly, and met his gaze.

'But there's very little we can add to that, I'm afraid. Your constable was already at the scene when we arrived. We were responding to his whistle.'

'Ah. Yes, well. If we're speaking frankly, you know as well as I do that the constable in question was just a boy. And an inexperienced boy at that. When I questioned him on the topic this morning, he said that you appeared to know a great deal about the victim and the manner in which the murder had occurred.'

Honoré glanced at Emily, unsure how much to give away.

'I was in the army for many years. I saw a lot of death, and I picked up a lot of experience in the field. I know how to evaluate a situation.'

'Ah, a military man.' Newman nodded, as if that statement alone explained away all his many questions. He turned back to Lechasseur.

'Honestly, what do you believe occurred in the alleyway in the moments before you arrived? I mean, have you any inkling as to who, or what, may have been responsible for making that *mess*?'

It was Honoré's turn to hesitate. 'Well, some sort of beast, obviously. But I'm sure it can't have been a dog. And then there's the fact that you keep referring to a killer. From that, I presume you are under the impression that whatever this beast is, it's being controlled by a man, a man who is targeting certain individuals, marking them out to be killed?'

'That's the line of enquiry we're currently pursuing, yes.' Newman inclined his head in affirmation..

'So, we're looking for a man with some sort of exotic beast or animal. There can't be that many of them in London at this time … at the moment. Is there a circus nearby, or a stage show?'

'Nothing.' Newman hesitated. 'But there is something else.'

He reached into the file and withdrew a small card, about the size of a typical playing card. He placed it face up on the surface of the desk in front of them. Emily reached over and picked it up.

When she saw the image on the front of the card, Emily dropped it with a sharp gasp.

Newman, feigning concern, took this in with an inquisitive interest. 'My dear, are you quite all right?'

Emily sat back and tried to steady herself.

Lechasseur reached over and picked the card off the floor, glancing at the picture as he did so. It was the image of a horned devil, sitting atop a pillar, its two subjugated human slaves naked and chained by its feet. Pentacles and other sinister runes and symbols adorned its semi-naked form. The image itself had an almost cartoon-like quality to it, as if it were some sort of terrible caricature, yet it nevertheless chilled Lechasseur, stirring something quiet and cold within him. He looked up at Newman and placed the card carefully back on the desk. 'Why are you showing us this?'

Newman caught his eye, before glancing back at Emily, who had shuffled around in her seat and was watching Honoré anxiously. 'Tarot.' He seemed to ignore Lechasseur's question completely. 'One of the so-called Greater Arcana. The Devil.' He watched Emily carefully to see if she reacted to that.

She remained steadfast.

'This appears to be his calling-card. The killer's, that is.' He paused for a moment. Lechasseur filled the gap.

'You mean, the killer leaves these at the scene of each murder to let you know he's responsible?'

'Indeed I do. We've found an identical card at the scene of each death, with the exception of the incident that occurred this morning … We're wondering if he was disturbed before he had time to place it.'

'Or if *we* were the ones placing the cards on the bodies.' Lechasseur snorted. 'Well, I can assure you that's not the case.'

'No, well …' Newman looked a little sheepish. 'You understand that I have to follow all lines of enquiry.'

There was a brief moment of awkwardness. Then Emily spoke in a quiet, even voice. 'Were the cards all left in the same place? I mean; did he leave them on the floor nearby, or on the body? I certainly didn't see anything when we stumbled upon the dead man in the alleyway last night.'

'Yes, indeed, they're always in the same place, clutched in the left hand of the victim. It's got the boys here a bit spooked, if truth be known. All this occult business, devil worshippers and whatnot. They're saying – amongst themselves – that the creature that's killing these poor chaps is some kind of devil spawn or diabolical beast. Fanciful, I know.' Newman shrugged, and then slipped the Tarot card back into the file.

Emily glanced at Lechasseur. Newman stood up from behind his desk.

'Anyway, thank you for all your assistance. If only there were more people like the two of you, willing to rally round when they hear a police whistle, we'd not be in the circumstances we're in today.'

Honoré looked at him wryly, rubbing his battered face. Newman stumbled, obviously embarrassed. 'Of course, we'll have to make sure that people are treated with a little more grace in future.' He smiled. 'Thank you both, once again. I'll have one of the lads show you out.' He moved to the door and opened it. 'I won't keep you a moment.'

Newman left the room, and, in a single smooth movement, Honoré swept the file towards him on the desk, opened it, and quickly started scanning the typewritten sheets therein. Emily glanced worriedly at the door, but after a moment, Honoré slid the sheets back in the file and replaced it in its original position on the table.

A moment later, Newman reappeared with a young man in a suit and tie.

'Johnson here will show you out. I've got a hundred and one things to be getting on with.'

Johnson turned towards Emily and Lechasseur, a slightly perplexed look on his face. 'If you'd like to follow me …' He turned about and started his way slowly along the corridor. Newman stepped around his desk and took Lechasseur's hand in his own. 'If you think of anything, you know where to find me.'

Lechasseur smiled. 'I certainly do. Thanks for the brandy.' He took Emily by the arm and, together, the two of them stepped out of the office and set off after the younger man in the suit.

As they were led away from Newman's office, Emily and Honoré exchanged a cautious glance. Emily reached out and placed a hand on Honoré's arm, urging him to slow down so they would drop out of earshot of the young officer.

'Honoré, about the tramp …'

Lechasseur put a finger to his lips. 'Not here, Emily. We'll be outside in a few moments. Let's go somewhere quiet.'

Emily nodded, obviously biting her tongue.

They continued on down a flight of stairs and out into the main foyer of the building. Through the glass panes that lined the walls, the sunlight was filtering in, creating great columns of dust and light that swirled in the air, pooling on the shiny-tiled surface of the floor. Men in uniform shuffled around the place like so many worker ants, the drone of their chattering voices combining to create a kind of deep, low-level hum.

Honoré and Emily made their way towards the exit, following the trail of the junior who had led them there from Newman's office. Just before the doors, he stopped them with a wave of his hand.

'You are free to go. Thank you for your cooperation. Please return the garments at your earliest opportunity.'

He sounded bored, delivering a line he had probably spoken a thousand times before. He stared forward into the middle distance, not even interested enough to watch them leave as they stepped out into the brisk morning and made their way, slowly, along the street and away from the vast police headquarters.

After a moment, Honoré hesitated, coming to a sudden halt. Emily skipped a few paces ahead of him before stopping herself and turning back to see what the problem was.

'Come on Hon …' Just as she was about to hurry him along, she followed the line of his gaze, to see Newman watching them from his window on the second floor, his face partially obscured by the sheen of light from the reflected sun.

Honoré shivered and turned about, taking Emily by the arm as he headed off along the street.

'Let's get out of here. I think I need a cup of tea.'

At that, Emily almost laughed out loud.

After a brief walk along the riverside, they came upon a small tearoom set back from the river amongst a number of smaller, ramshackle buildings. They ducked inside, and were immediately assaulted by the smell of frying bacon and eggs. Lechasseur felt his stomach lurch. He turned to Emily. 'Find us a table at the back. I'll order us some food.'

'But what about …?'

'Don't worry. I'll take care of it.'

Emily shrugged and wandered over to a table in the corner of the room, shook off her coat and pulled up a seat. She felt rather odd sitting there in a long, Victorian dress, and rather constricted too, but no-one else seemed to think she looked out of place. Honoré, on the other hand, had certainly been drawing a few looks whilst they made their way through the busier streets. It was quiet in the little tearoom, however, and the few patrons that were around were sat hunched over their morning papers, or else staring through the grimy windows at the riverfront, watching the world go by. They were too wrapped up in their own thoughts to allow their attention to be distracted even by something as unusual as a tall black man accompanied by a pretty young woman.

After a moment, Honoré appeared at the edge of the table with a small tray. A large pot of tea, a jug of milk and two china cups were placed in front of her on the table, before he slid into the seat opposite and removed his own coat, hanging it over the back of his chair.

'Food will be over shortly.' He reached over and poured himself a drink.

Emily looked at him quizzically. 'Where did you get the money from?'

'Ah. I've been meaning to get to that …' He reached into his pocket and drew out a small black wallet of beaten leather, which he placed on the table before her.

Emily turned it over in her hand. It was well worn and emblazoned in gilt with the initials E G.

'I figured he wouldn't be needing it any more.' Honoré smiled. 'Besides, I thought we needed to know who he was.'

Emily looked aghast, and placed the wallet back on the table. 'You took that from the corpse? Last night? Put it away, Honoré, I don't want to know any more.'

'Come on Emily, there's more to it than that. I saw something last night that I think we need to investigate.'

'Okay. Okay. But first let me tell you about the tramp.'

'I need to tell you about what I saw.'

'I understand that Honoré, but this is important too!'

'Look …' He paused whilst the waitress placed two plates of bacon and eggs on the table in front of them. 'Let's eat our breakfast first and then we can both tell each other what's on our minds.' He picked up his knife and fork and started cutting into his bacon.

Emily waited until he had taken a mouthful of food before launching into her monologue.

'Right. You eat, I'll talk. I've been thinking about that tramp all night and I think I've got an answer, of sorts. Consider this: how old was the man we saw in 1950?'

Honoré looked at her in desperation, before mouthing his reply around his food. 'About late thirties, thirty-five?'

'Exactly. So how could we have followed his timeline all the way back to 1892?'

Honoré sat up, placing his cutlery down on the edge of his plate. He considered that for a moment whilst he swallowed his food. 'What are you saying?'

'I'm saying that he must be a time traveller like you or me. Think about it. He's alive, here, somewhere, in a period well before he could possibly have even been born. And the fact that his timeline is all broken and severed, that must mean something, must have something to do with his connection to time. If you think about it, that's why he could have been showing you images of me in your dream. Maybe trying to tell you that he was like me? Perhaps he needs your help to make a jump in time, or something.'

Lechasseur looked a little startled. 'Why didn't I think of that? It's all so obvious. And it fits in, somehow, with what I need to tell you.'

'Which is?'

'The dead man, Edward Groves,' Honoré waved the wallet at her to emphasise the point, 'was a time sensitive too. Or I think so, anyway. His time-snake was *different*, suggestive. I don't believe he was active in the same way as you or I, but I do think there has to be a link there somewhere.'

Emily sounded shocked. 'You don't think the tramp is the murderer, do you? That *would* explain why he was present in this time period, and why he was looking for you in 1950.'

Honoré levelled his gaze at her. He looked suddenly serious.

Emily shuddered and reached out for her tea, trying to reassure herself with a long, hot draught.

'I don't know, Emily, I really don't. But I suppose it's going to be up to us to find out.'

'So what's next? After the bacon and eggs, I mean?' Emily had made a start on her breakfast while Lechasseur was talking.

'We visit the scene of the most recent murder.' He smiled.

'You got the address from Newman's file?'

'Yeah. And I've got a horrible feeling we're not going to like what we find.'

The walk across town took about forty-five minutes. The layout of the streets and buildings was vaguely familiar to Lechasseur, yet every time he was confident he knew exactly where he was going, he'd turn down a side street and end up lost. The city refused to give up its secrets.

The day was gusty and overcast, and although it was not yet raining, it felt like it was holding back, ready for a downpour. That, in itself, felt a little portentous, and left Honoré feeling broody and tired.

As they walked, Honoré tried to piece it all together in his head. If the severed man *was* the murderer, then they were on the trail of a killer; and not only that, but a killer who was looking for him, too. To what end, he could only imagine.

His gut instinct, however, suggested something different entirely. He just didn't believe that the tramp was trying to kill him. If that had been the case, he'd have made his move by now, probably in 1950, when Lechasseur had been less aware of what was going on and more vulnerable because of his ignorance. It had to be something else.

But what? Where was the connection he was missing? If the tramp had travelled here from the future, there had to be a reason. And somehow that had to tie in with the deaths. He was sure of it. Particularly after discovering that Edward Groves had been a time sensitive like himself. And then there was the fact that the tramp had been severed from his own timeline, yet still existed within at least two, probably three time periods. He could make no real sense of all these disparate threads.

It all hinged, he supposed, on whether or not they would find anything at the scene of the second murder – a run-down apartment building over in the East End.

When they finally arrived, after spending some time exploring the area, they found the house had been boarded up. It was a tall tenement building, nestled amongst a number of other rather run-down looking flats and shops. The police had obviously decided to move on, and Lechasseur could see signs of forced entry in the building next door. It certainly didn't look like the sort of place they wanted to hang around in for too long.

Emily had obviously had the same thought. 'Are you sure we've got the right place, Honoré? It looks a bit ... well, a bit like an uninhabited slum.'

'It's the right place. The boards on the windows look new and it's certainly the correct address.' Honoré edged his way over towards the front door and tested the lock. The police had done a good job barricading the door, and it wouldn't give.

'I think we're going to have to get in round the back. Come on, this way.'

They circled their way around the small terrace and ducked down an alleyway at the back. A pervasive stench assailed them, and Emily walked carefully around slops of mess and rotting food waste that had been dumped on the cobbles, unwanted. A scruffy-looking black cat was sniffing around amongst the rubbish, looking for a scrap of something half-edible. It scampered away when it noticed them coming.

The back gate gave way easily to Honoré's shoulder whilst Emily kept watch, and they stepped into the overgrown yard at the rear of the property. It was clear almost immediately that the place had been more-or-less abandoned for some time; weeds rose out of the ground from between the paving slabs like miniature eruptions of green and yellow, the hope of life from deep amongst the detritus. More rubbish was piled into the corners of the yard; old, burnt-out pieces of furniture, a chair here, a table there. Lechasseur thought he could even see the edge of an old oil painting sticking out from the flowerbed, half burnt away and turned into so much useless carbon and ash. The place had an oppressive air about it, and both Honoré and Emily were keen to keep moving before it settled on them and took hold. They clambered over the stacks of waste and made their way towards the sash window at the back of the house. The police had not even bothered to attempt to board up the rear, probably assuming that the stacks of rubbish would be enough of a deterrent to any would-be thieves. Either that or they had more important things to do, like beating up innocent civilians. Lechassuer rubbed his bruised face with a painful cringe.

Emily was looking at the bricked-up hole where the back door had once been. 'Looks like someone was keen to keep other people out.'

'Or to keep people in.' Honoré gave Emily an ominous glance. 'We'll get in through this window here. Come on, pass me that.' He indicated amongst the rubbish, and Emily dug out a rusty metal bar that looked as if it had once been part of an old iron bed frame. Honoré used it to prise open the window, which crumbled away almost immediately, obviously rotten through. He pushed the frame up on its runners, wincing at the loud creaking sound it made, and beckoned for Emily to climb inside.

'What, me first?

'Why not?'

'In this dress?'

'Okay, I'll go.' He swung one leg up onto the windowsill, careful to balance his weight so that the crumbling wooden frame wouldn't give way beneath him. A moment later, he lifted himself bodily through the hole and disappeared into the darkness of the old house. To Emily, it seemed disconcertingly like he'd just been swallowed. She heard his feet land on the other side with a resounding crunch.

He was quiet for a moment whilst he looked around.

Emily was almost startled when, a minute later, his head emerged from the window again, smiling. 'Come on in, it looks okay.' He reached out and took her hands, helping her up.

She landed beside him with a thud.

The room in which they found themselves was dark and small, but with a high ceiling that gave the place a kind of eerie vastness, making Emily feel more than a little uncomfortable. It was as if it reminded her of somewhere, some familiar location that she just couldn't place. Piles of rubbish and paper were spread around all over the floor.

Every movement that they made seemed amplified by the unnatural silence of the old house. Emily felt the tiny hairs on the back of her neck bristle.

'This place is so quiet. There was never any love here.'

Honoré knew exactly what she meant; there was a terrible atmosphere of loneliness, of isolation, like they were somewhere otherworldly, somewhere at odds with the real world. Given his experiences of late, nothing would surprise him less.

'I'm going to take a look upstairs. You check it out down here.'

'What if I find the body?' Emily's nervousness was evident in her voice.

'They'll have moved it by n ...' Lechasseur, half turned towards Emily, stopped dead in mid-sentence. Emily had the sense that he had taken a step backwards away from her.

'Honoré? What is it, Honoré?'

Nothing.

Emily could feel her palms getting sweaty. Her heart raced in her chest. She stepped forward into the shaft of light that was streaming in from the window, trying to pick out Lechasseur from amongst the shadows. 'What's the matter, Honoré?'

It took him a moment to answer, and to Emily, it seemed like an age.

'I'm here.' His voice seemed to echo from across the room.

'What happened?'

'Nothing. I'm going to head upstairs now.'

'Honoré! You can't do that! You can't just freak out like that and then say nothing. Not here. Not in this horrible house.' She sounded like she was about to explode with frustration.

Honoré stepped forward and placed a hand on her arm. His face was still shrouded in the darkness. 'We're okay, Emily. Everything's okay. Let's get this over with and get out of here as soon as we can.' He stepped back and moved away, his feet crunching on the rubbish that littered the floor all around them.

A moment later, Emily heard the sound of his boots echoing on the wooden staircase as he made his way up to the next floor.

She was alone in the darkness again. Thoughts began to spiral through her mind. She could see things coming out of the gloom.

The Devil was there in all his terrible regalia, taunting her, his red eyes burning out of the blackness. Like the image on the Tarot card, he sat atop a marble pillar, his hoofed foot clacking against its smoothly-polished surface as he impatiently tapped out a rhythm like a tortured, mesmerising heartbeat. He was watching her, waiting for her to make a move. Emily whimpered and shook her head, closing her eyes, willing the image to disappear.

For a moment, everything was darkness once again.

Then the face of the severed man erupted out of nowhere, feverish, silently imploring her, begging her to carry out some dreadful task.

She screamed and ran from the room, calling for Lechasseur,

scrabbling awkwardly in the darkness for the staircase. In seconds, Honoré was by her side, ready for whatever had scared her.

'What is it? Where?' He was frantic, fired up with adrenaline and concern.

Emily grabbed for him in the dark until she caught his arm. She pulled him close, holding him quietly for a moment. When she spoke, it was barely a whisper.

'It's this house. Something horrific happened here, Honoré, something truly, truly awful. The building's full of terror.'

'I know.' He paused for a moment, then wrapped his arm around her shoulders. 'I've just found what we were looking for. I think you'd better come take a look.'

Cautiously, they made their way up the staircase, Honoré leading Emily by the hand, the steps creaking loudly beneath their weight. When they reached the top, Lechasseur came to rest on the small landing and turned towards her. 'Are you up to this?'

'How bad is it?'

'It's … not what I was expecting. The body's gone. But there's something else, something that makes me think that we were on the right tracks when we said we thought the murders had some sort of connection to time.'

'What?'

Honoré reached out and opened the door behind her, which Emily had hardly even noticed in the dark.

'Take a look.'

She stepped inside. And gasped.

The room was full of clocks.

They were everywhere, covering every surface, filling every single space on every wall. Each of them was different from the others; some small and ornate in gold or silver casings, some as large as grandfather clocks, exquisitely carved out of the finest mahogany. Pocket watches hung from the ceiling like tiny, sparkling stars, dangling on their chains to create a varied and strangely beautiful timescape suspended above the entire room. Carriage clocks sat proudly on the naked floorboards amongst piles of paper and torn bedclothes.

It was the sound that got to Emily first, however; the aural assault of so many timepieces ticking together in such a tiny space; all out of sync with one another, all attempting to measure time in a manner slightly at odds with their counterparts. It was as if the whole of history was present in this little room, every second being counted over and over again *ad infinitum*; a war of time fought out in an East End flat in Victorian London.

Emily wanted to press her hands to her ears and make it all stop. The ticking was like a strange sort of music, an out-of-step dance, and in her mind's eye she could see the image of the Devil again, tapping his foot to the strangely rhythmic beating of the clocks, searching through the time zones with his piercing red eyes, looking for paths amongst the chaos.

And as if that wasn't enough, Emily noted, there was a large, corpse-sized space amongst the clocks on the floor; a space spattered with blood and gore; the results of whatever had happened to the occupier of this extraordinary, terrifying room. A number of the artefacts on the floor had apparently been overturned or smashed in the fight.

Emily turned back to Lechasseur, who was standing in the doorway behind her.

'Honoré. What are you thinking?'

'That something very strange and very horrible is going on here.'

Emily shivered. 'I figured that much out myself.'

Honoré edged a little further into the room and reached out, plucking something from within the mechanism of one of the taller grandfather clocks that stood against the wall to her left. He held it up for Emily to see in the dim light.

A Tarot card. She took it from him and examined it more closely. It was identical to the one she had seen in Newman's office just a few hours earlier. She handed it back to Honoré, who caught her eye, before slipping it into his pocket.

'So, Emily, want to tell me what's going on?'

She looked at him, stunned for a moment. 'What do you mean?'

'I mean the thing with you and this Devil card. I saw the reaction you had to it in Newman's office. And then there was that thing with the stagecoach that nearly bowled us over when we arrived.' He looked confused, and more than a little frustrated. 'What is it that you're not telling me? What do you know about what's going on?'

'That's just it! I don't know anything! I just keep seeing these horrible pictures of the Devil, and they terrify me, Honoré, really, really terrify me.' He could see in the darkness that she had started to cry. 'I don't know what's the matter with me, but I keep having these dreams, these visions of the Devil, sitting on top of a marble pillar like the one in the picture. Every time I close my eyes, I can see him looking back at me, staring right at me, as if he's looking for something or searching me out in the darkness. It's like I'm lost and he's trying to find me. And the thing is, I don't know what's real and what's not anymore!' At this, she broke down into sobs and covered her face with her hands, trying to stem the flow of tears. Lechasseur stepped towards her, put his arm around her shoulders and held her tightly.

'It's all right Emily. You're just tired, that's all. I guess neither of us has had much sleep recently, and all these horrible events are finally starting to get to you. It's just your mind playing tricks on you, same thing that's been happening to me.'

Emily pushed back from him, suddenly hesitant. 'What do you mean?'

'You know, dreams and stuff. Seeing things in the darkness. It's just your head's way of telling you to slow down, to take a rest. We've been through a lot in the last couple of days, that's all.'

'Is that what happened downstairs – seeing things in the darkness?'

Honoré shrugged. 'Yeah, I guess so.' He turned to walk away, heading out of the room.

Emily tried to catch him. 'What did you see?'

'It was nothing.'

'Tell me, Honoré. I'm not a child.'

He stopped and looked back at her, plainly unsure whether to say anything or not.

'Honoré …'

'Okay.' He levelled his gaze on her. 'When I looked at you, you were standing there in the corner, staring right back at me.'

'And …?'

'And you had a Devil's head.' A pause. 'Now come on, let's get out of this godforsaken place and find somewhere quiet to get some rest.'

Emily, without saying another word, followed him down the rickety staircase and carefully around the piles of rubbish and grime towards the blinding daylight outside.

BLOOD, DEATH AND MORTAR

He was standing behind a low wall, watching, waiting.

Honoré could hear his own breath whistling out between his pursed lips as he attempted to ignore the cold. In the distance, he could hear the sound of gunfire; shells howling through the still air, explosions creating pock-marks in the surface of the world, throwing clods of dirt and bits of men up into the air like so many scattered seeds on the wind.

He gripped his rifle and waited. Beside him, one of his fellow soldiers was lighting up a cigarette, his back placed precariously to the wall. Honoré had seen this before; a bullet in the back of the head when you weren't looking. That's what became of careless men in this war. The enemy didn't think twice about shooting you in the back.

Still, one shell in the wrong place and they'd all be swimming in dirt and blood anyhow.

He glanced around warily. The farmhouse was a shattered ruin. It loomed behind them, casting wide, sweeping shadows in the bright sunlight and serving as a cover against the rapid enemy fire. Lechasseur supposed that it must have been destroyed some time in the recent past, at least since the onset of the war, although there was no obvious evidence of any blast or explosion. Just the broken, crumbled remains of the old stone house and the remnants of a barn that had collapsed in on itself and was now completely useless to them, even as cover.

Honoré heard a sudden, high-pitched wail as a shell screamed overhead, bursting into light and flame where it touched the ground just a few hundred yards behind them. He looked around at his fellows to see most of them on the floor, rifles by their sides, sighing in relief that the enemy bomb had sailed so easily overhead.

All of them knew the dark death that awaited them, sometime in this dismal war, and all of them wanted to cheat it for as long as they humanly could.

Honoré looked out over the fields around the farm. Bizarrely, everything looked calm. If he concentrated, he could shut out the sounds of the shells and the screams and just see the rolling hills in the distance, the beautiful and unspoiled Normandy countryside. Then his eyes came to rest on the enemy stronghold in the neighbouring farm, and reality came flooding back to him with a start.

The encampment had been fenced off with a tangled web of barbed wire, and the ground churned into a sodden mess by the wheels of the supply vehicles. Gun emplacements lined the edges of the camp, and Honoré could see figures moving about like tiny ants. Every few minutes, one of the artillery guns would go off and another shell would fly howling overhead.

He crouched down, resting the barrel of his rifle against the wall for a moment. The other men had returned to their positions and were joking with each other about another near miss. It was their way of trying to deal with the constant threat of death, but Lechasseur found it difficult to join in. To him, death was no laughing matter. For weeks, he'd been seeing ghosts wandering about on the battlefields; the dead come back to life to stalk the living.

He'd already decided he was going crazy; or, at least, that the war was getting to him in ways he hadn't expected, starting to inspire hallucinations and moments of bizarre lucidity in which he was sure he was seeing what was *really* there … only to decide, moments later, that it had all been a figment of his vivid imagination.

He thought back to the last time it had happened, just a couple of days before.

It was early in the morning, and most of the other men were just beginning to stir, packing up their sleeping bags in the old farmhouse and trying to manufacture some form of breakfast from the measly rations they had left at the bottom of their packs. Lechasseur had been on watch for a few hours, hidden in the foliage on the outskirts of their encampment. It had been a quiet night, with little enemy activity, and he had allowed himself to relax, resting his rifle alongside him in the bushes. The sun was just beginning to filter in from the East, swirling away the light mist that had settled over the fields during the night like some ethereal blanket. He glanced up momentarily, just to scan the area before beginning preparations to return to camp. And that's when he saw them.

Thousands of people, all walking towards him out of the mist, marching ominously and silently towards something he couldn't see. It was as if the entire enemy army had just mobilised and appeared in front of him in the time it had taken him to blink and look away.

He frowned and scrabbled to reclaim his rifle, clambering to his knees in the dirt. He'd have to make a run for it, inform the others to pull back before the enemy stormed the camp. He had no idea how so many people could have got so close without him noticing.

He looked back. The figures were drawing closer now, and he could see some of their faces. They looked like *civilians*. But the strangest thing was what was going on in the spaces *between* them. It was as if the mist had rolled in with the tides of people, as if the rows and rows of these strange apparitions were surrounded by some sort of distortion, some sort of *wave* of mist that warped his view of them and caused him to feel dizzy and disorientated.

And, most bizarrely of all, one of the figures at the head of the procession appeared to be female and wearing a pair of pink, silken pyjamas. The nightclothes fluttered around her body, revealing stretches of pale leg and the shape of her hips and breasts ... But the figure bore the head of a horned devil, not that of a human being.

He raised his rifle and took a shot.

The rows of people continued to march on regardless, not even turning to look.

He aimed again, drawing a bead on the strange devil creature.

His shot seemed to pass right through it, as if it wasn't really there.

The figure came to a halt. For a moment, it stood there in the misty field, whilst the press of people just seemed to swarm around it, unperturbed. Then it turned and looked directly at him, it eyes glowing a glassy, fiery red.

Lechasseur didn't hesitate a moment longer. He turned and ran, leaving his rifle lying on the ground amongst the fallen leaves, and didn't stop running until he'd cleared the camp and was standing in the middle of a field alone, panting at the empty sky.

Somewhere in the distance he heard the howl of an animal, and wondered if it was actually something else entirely ...

Honoré woke in a cold sweat.

He sat bolt upright on the bed, looking around in the dark. Emily was still asleep on the other side of the room, curled up on her tiny bunk. The room stank of stale sweat and urine.

He rubbed his face with his hands. He had to do something about these dreams; they were starting to affect his ability to keep his mind on the job. Not only that, but he was sure they were starting to impact upon his relationship with Emily. Something was going on behind the scenes, and he was sure it had a lot to do with the images that kept cropping up in his nightmares.

But there was more than that, too. Now he was beginning to doubt the veracity of his own memory. What was real and what was not? He remembered clearly the moment in Normandy when he had seen all those walking, spectral figures, and at the time had put it down to sheer fatigue and a deep-seated weariness with the War. Later, after discovering his bizarre sensitivity to time, he had looked back on a number of oddities from his past in a new light, and had seen them in the context of his new life. The 'ghosts' had probably been figures from different time zones, all interweaving with one another, crossing each other's paths, centuries apart. It had simply been his unfiltered mind that had allowed him to see it all at once, provided him with a rare 'overview' of time; and it had nearly driven him insane in the process.

He had learned to live with these surrealistic visions by simply blanking them out, shutting out the strange real-world he could see and forcing himself to lead what he figured was a 'normal' life. After a while it had become a reflex, a lowering of the shades to keep out the nightmares on the other side of the window. Until he had gone and gotten himself mixed up in the 'Emily Blandish' affair, that is ...

He tried to cast his mind back to that time on the embankment in Normandy. Now, in the cold light of day, he couldn't recall seeing the Emily/Devil figure amongst the others in the field, nor remember actually shooting at any of the people in the strange, ethereal crowd. Was that a figment of his dream, or was there something far more sinister going on, something that was starting to draw elements from his past further and further into the present day? Had all this been working away in the background for years, toiling like some devilish mechanism that was drawing, patiently, towards some terrible and unexpected endgame? If so, it looked like things were going to come to a head soon enough. Honoré could feel the tension like a palpable, electric field in the air, and it was starting to get to him, to wear him down.

He felt lost, isolated, and aware that the one person he could talk to about all this was the one person he needed to talk *about*. The irony almost made him laugh out loud.

Honoré climbed off the bed and found his coat and boots in the half-light. Emily stirred briefly on the nearby bunk, but he froze in the doorway, and after a moment she rolled over and continued to doze. She looked peaceful lying there, resting. Honoré felt guilty leaving her by herself, but he needed to get some air. Alone.

With one last glance at Emily, he slipped out of the door to their room, stepped quietly onto the landing of the boarding house and then onwards down the stairs and away.

Outside, the night was like a purple stain; the sky was under-lit by a brilliant wash of bronzes and deep reds. Yellow fog curled around every corner, hugging the ground and clinging to the air like some sort of vaporous, airborne leech.

Honoré pulled his coat tight around himself and tried to get his bearings, looking around for a building or sign he could easily place. He wanted to be back before Emily woke, and the thought of getting lost in the soupy fog was not at all appealing. He glanced up and down the street, looking to see if there was anybody else about. The place seemed deserted.

He set out, passing under a small bridge and following the road as it curled around to the left, stretching away into the fog-filled night. He had no real idea where he was going; he just intended to walk until he felt the air of oppression lifting, or else he managed to get a clear perspective on his current predicament. It wasn't that he didn't *trust* Emily. It was more that he felt she was holding back on something. Whether or not she was even aware of that herself was something else that had crossed his mind.

With Emily, he was beginning to learn, everything eventually came back to her amnesia, and the fact she simply *couldn't* remember what she did and didn't know.

Honoré ducked down a deserted side street, past a public house that still stank of spilt beer – even though it had obviously been closed for hours – and then round into a small park that sat neatly in the middle of one of London's old residential squares. During his time in the city, albeit many years in the future, Lechasseur had come to know this type of setup well; he had often found himself venturing into these parts of the city during his time as a spiv, sitting amongst the leafy foliage in the middle of a small park, observing the comings and goings at one of the local houses, or else tracking the movements of a mildly interesting criminal or over-zealous lover.

He didn't really miss that kind of minutiae, the details of others people's lives, but he did miss the long stretches of time spent on his own, just sitting there, watching the world go by.

He made a beeline for a nearby bench and sat down, dusting off the seat with the edge of his sleeve to make sure he wasn't going to get covered in grime. The fog was heavy and damp, curling around the surrounding plants in long wisps and hiding everything from view. It made him think of Normandy once again, and he shivered, despite his warm clothing.

He stuck his hands down deep in his coat pockets to savour their warmth. The fingers of his right hand encountered something shoved up against the lining, and he pulled on it, trying to get it free. When he did, he was disappointed to see that it was only the Tarot card he had taken from the murder scene earlier that day. He dropped it on the floor by his feet. When he looked back at it a moment later, the Devil was staring up at him, a cruel yet charming smile upon his face. Honoré looked away again. Somehow, the Devil seemed to have a hand in his business at the moment. To what end, he still wasn't sure.

He sat there for about an hour, gazing into the fog, trying to look for answers in the empty night. He didn't see or hear from another soul until a police whistle went off loudly nearby and he knew, all of a sudden, that they'd just found evidence of another horrific murder, and that things were either going to become suddenly very clear, or else unravel about him like a loose thread pulled maliciously tight.

Lechasseur didn't wait for the whistle to sound again. He was on his feet in a moment, running quickly towards the scene of the disturbance. Somehow, in the back of his mind, he could see clearly what he was going to find: another young police officer out of his depth, another bloody corpse, another Tarot card of the grinning devil, and another mystery to add to his growing pile of problems. He doubted Sherlock Holmes had ever had quite so many things to deal with at once.

He reached the point where he believed the whistle had come from, a crossroads of old cobbled roads.

Nothing.

He stood for a moment, spinning around on the spot, trying to decide which direction to take. The fog swirled around him, pressing against his skin like a damp compress. He couldn't make out exactly where he was.

He cursed, exasperated, and decided to wait for the whistle to sound again so he could follow its signal. He was sure he couldn't be that far away.

Then, to Honoré's surprise, he heard the sound of a hoof clacking loudly against the cobbles behind him. He turned around hesitantly, not sure what he was expecting to see. He couldn't help conjuring up the image of the Devil in his mind; a tall, dark, grinning figure that would emerge from the damp fog with piercing red eyes.

He braced himself and faced his adversary nervously. The gloomy fog was shrouding everything, closing in on Honoré and making it difficult to see. Then, all of a sudden, the fog seemed to part like a curtain, and two horses emerged from the wall of grey, their nostrils steaming in the cold night, a rambling carriage trailing behind them like some sort of ancient black chariot. They were heading straight for him, and if it hadn't been for the rain of hooves pounding at the stonework, he would have thought they were floating; they glided so quickly and easily toward him. He dived out of the way, landing hard on his shoulder, and managed to roll around to get a look at his opponent as the carriage swung around. A man was crouched hard over the reins of the horses on the front of the carriage, driving them on. His face was hidden beneath a dark cloak, and Honoré could see a shining whistle dangling on a chain from his wrist. Had he lured Honoré here to attempt to run him down?

The carriage sped off into the fog, and again, for the second time in as many days, Honoré caught a glimpse of a strange red symbol on the side of it, a symbol that now looked decidedly like it was intended to represent a horned creature of some sort.

He also noted, as it passed him by, a terrible whining and scrabbling sound from inside the carriage itself, as if there was some sort of animal penned up inside it.

He scrambled to his feet and quickly checked himself over. Just as he was about to take off after the carriage, he heard a voice scream out behind him.

'Honoré! Stop!'

It was Emily, and she sounded desperate, hollow and distraught. He turned around. She was standing behind him, holding her hands out towards him, palms turned upwards, tears rolling down her cheeks like trickling rivers of salt.

Her hands were covered in blood.

'He's dead. He's dead. He's dead.'

Lechasseur was stunned. For a moment he didn't respond, and Emily just continued to stagger towards him, gore dripping from her outstretched hands. He took a step towards her, and then stepped back again, unsure.

'Emily, who's dead?'

She didn't respond.

This time his voice was firmer. 'Who's dead, Emily?'

She looked up at him, imploring with her eyes. 'I don't know!'

'Are *you* okay?'

'I couldn't keep him alive, Honoré. I couldn't keep him alive …' She trailed off into a series of heartfelt sobs, and Lechasseur felt himself softening, stepping towards her, holding her face as she cried. He didn't know what to make of the blood.

After a couple of minutes had passed in silence, she led him back to where she had found the dying man, just a moment's walk away from where he had been.

The corpse was a bloody mess, and it was clear that Emily had tried to pump the man's chest in an attempt to keep him alive. It had obviously been a futile gesture; his throat had been torn away in the vicious assault, and the sheer amount of blood suggested to Honoré that the man had not died easily. He tried to see what was left of the face.

It certainly wasn't the severed man.

He handed Emily a handkerchief from his pocket. 'Come on. You did everything you possibly could. Clean yourself up as best you can and let's get out of here before the police arrive. I think we could both do without spending another night in the cells.'

Emily, still sobbing, mopped her hands ineffectually on the handkerchief and dropped it on the floor beside the body. They started off, heading in the same direction as the carriage.

'What are you … Hang on.' Lechasseur turned and ran back to the body. He knelt over the dead man momentarily and rummaged in his pockets. A minute later he was back beside Emily, brandishing an old, worn Tarot card. Emily wouldn't even look at it.

Honoré slipped it safely into his pocket. He knew now, with a growing certainty, that the mysterious carriage held the secret to the series of murders that had been plaguing the city – and, more precisely, the time sensitive people who seemed to be active in this period. He knew also that whoever was responsible for those murders was aware of him and Emily, and certainly didn't have their best interests at heart. Once again, it appeared to come down to their rare connection to time. Somehow, the murderer could see this in a very tangible way, and was hunting them out, stalking them – almost teasing them – as they went around the city, following his footsteps.

But why had he spared Lechasseur, after luring him to the scene just a few minutes earlier? The driver could have easily reined in the horses and taken another attempt to run him down. But instead, he had just disappeared into the night. Something was nagging at the back of Lechasseur's mind.

He turned to Emily, who was trailing behind him, her face to the floor.

'What were you doing out here? I thought I left you asleep in bed?'

'I woke up when you were moving about in the room.'

'Then why didn't you say something?'

'I wanted to see what you were up to. Why you were poking about on your own. I didn't expect you to sit in the park for an hour.'

Honoré shook his head. 'I just wanted some time alone. I needed some space, some time to think things through and take stock of what's been going on. I didn't want you to feel excluded. It's just ...' He trailed off.

'Just what?'

'It's just that you seem to know more about what's going on than I do. Why are you so freaked out by all this Devil stuff?'

'We've been through this, Honoré. I *don't* know any more than you do. If anything, I have even less idea about what's been going on than you! I have no memories of anything to do with the Devil. Perhaps there was something that happened in the past, some body-memory that makes me react in the way I do, but I really don't have any concept of how that interacts with what we're doing here. I'm sorry, Honoré, but I'm finding this just as hard as you are. All this blood and death ...' She held her bloodstained hands up to him and shrugged.

Lechasseur was unsure how to respond. Just as he was about to say something, he stopped suddenly and indicated for Emily to stay still. They both listened. Somewhere nearby, hidden by the fog, were a couple of horses, whinnying with pent up energy. Honoré tried to ascertain which direction the sound was coming from.

A moment later, he looked round at Emily and pointed down a nearby side street.

'Down there.'

They fixed each other with a serious look.

'That coach we saw when we first arrived,' continued Honoré. 'It just tried to run me over again.'

Emily looked a little taken aback. 'You mean the coach that went past after I found the dying man? That was the same coach that nearly hit us when we first got here?'

'Yeah. I think the driver was the one who blew the whistle. He may have been trying to distract me, or else get my attention so he could try and run me down. Something startled him and he shot off. I was going to give chase when you showed up …' Lechasseur cocked his head to one side as if something had just struck him. 'It was *you*!'

'What do you mean, it was me?' Emily took a step back. 'I didn't do anything.'

'No. I mean, it was *you* who startled him so he ran away. He must have seen you coming and decided he couldn't take on two of us at once.' Honoré smiled. 'That's another one I owe you. Anyway, let's take a look. If he's stopped down here, we can try and surprise him.'

They slipped down the deserted street, edging their way along the front of the buildings to avoid being seen. Presently, they drew up next to a coaching inn that appeared to be still open for business. The lights were turned down low in the windows, but the sound of chatter could be heard coming from inside. Most of the rest of the street was quiet and empty, with just the sounds of the odd wakeful person rattling about in their house, or the occasional bark of a dog in the alleyways behind the buildings on the other side of the road.

Honoré shuffled cautiously into the yard at the rear of the old inn. Sure enough, two dark horses were tied to metal railings at the back of the area, drinking from a wide trough full of rainwater. Behind them, parked further into the yard, was the black coach they were looking for, the strange red symbol emblazoned brightly on its side. The whole place stank of dirt and manure. He beckoned to Emily, who was by his side a moment later.

'Let's see if we can find somewhere for you to clean up properly, and we can try and find out what's happened to the driver.'

'Okay. But why don't we wait and try to follow him back to wherever he's going?' Emily smiled. 'If we can find out where his base is …'

'Good idea. Let's see if there's a way in around the back.' They continued to edge their way into the yard. At the sight of the large American, the two horses began shuffling their feet and panting noisily, but Honoré slipped past them quickly, and they soon returned to the water, if a little more nervously than before.

Once he was sure there was no-one else around, Honoré made his way over to the parked coach. He circled it once, then stood beside Emily and looked it over.

It was a tatty old thing; nearing the end of its days as a useful transport. The wheels were old and starting to crack, and the frame of the carriage itself was splintered and tired. Nevertheless, someone had a use for it, and it was obvious to Honoré that they weren't concerned about the overall presentation; this was not a coach that was used to ferry around noblemen.

Emily was entirely enthralled by the sight of the red symbol, and had begun shaking again, as if it were bearing down on her, threatening to swallow her whole. Honoré guided her gently out of the way, trying not to dwell on her bizarre reaction. He wondered what was going on in her mind. He made sure she was okay, then edged around the side of the carriage and tried the door.

Locked.

He leaned up close, straining to try to hear if there was anything inside. He thought he could hear breathing – a ragged, rasping drawing of breath – on the other side of the door, and rapped his knuckles against the panel, trying to provoke a response.

'Hello? Is there anybody in there?'

Nothing.

'Hello?'

Suddenly the entire carriage *lurched* towards him, as whatever was inside abruptly shifted its weight and violently launched itself against the other side of the door. At the same time, the creature emitted a terrifying shriek; a wail so human and yet so animal that Honoré simply staggered backwards in shock and lost his footing. He scrabbled to catch himself from jarring his elbows sharply on the cobbles as he fell backward to the ground.

Emily ran over and helped him up.

'What the hell …?'

There was a commotion from inside the inn. The creature in the carriage was still wailing, a horrible, piercing, warbling noise that sounded more like a cry for help than anything intentionally confrontational. The coach itself was rocking from side to side as the animal threw itself around inside, banging off the walls like some kind of penned up beast. The horses were spooked now and were pulling on their chains, kicking out with their front legs and trying to bolt.

Honoré and Emily ran quickly into what appeared to be an outside store, and hid themselves behind a stack of barrels. They crouched low beside each other, and could just make out what was going on through a crack in the old brickwork.

The man in the hooded cloak came storming out of inn, another, stocky man trailing behind him, looking scared. Honoré took this second man to be the barkeep.

The hooded man produced a long stick or staff from under his cloak and rapped hard on the side of the carriage. When he spoke, his voice was a croaking rasp.

'Shut up in there!' He rapped again on the door. The creature inside emitted a low growl, that soon turned into a kind of strangled bark when the rapping continued. It knew its master's voice, and it didn't like it. 'Mind yourself, you miserable spawn of shit. I don't want to have to come in there and beat you again.' The growling stopped short. Obviously it knew its master well, and knew that he would make good on such threats.

Emily put her hand on Lechasseur's shoulder and whispered in his ear: 'What do you think they've got in there?'

Honoré took a moment to answer; he was busy watching the barkeep retreating quietly into the doorway, standing back from the fray. The horses were still making a cacophony of noise, stamping their hooves and whinnying loudly in fright.

He turned towards her, noticing the gleam reflected in her eyes from the shafts of moonlight that punctuated the thick fog. She had a smear of blood across her forehead where she had obviously wiped her brow in the heat of the moment during her attempts to save the murdered man.

'From the sounds of it, I'd say it was some sort of feral human, a wild boy or a tortured child of some sort. The Victorians used to bring them back from Africa or South America and display them in travelling shows. They probably beat the poor thing senseless and locked him in a cupboard for years, treating him like an animal.'

'Why?'

'Who knows, but I'm guessing it's got something to do with the murders. And that symbol; I think it must be connected to a devil-worshipping cult or something. It looks like a pair of horns.'

By now, the hooded man had calmed the scared horses and was making his way back towards the inn.

Emily appeared lost in thought. 'So what's this got to do with the severed man? Do you think he's mixed up in all this?'

'Without a doubt. But in what capacity, I'm still not sure. What I do know is that there's more to these murders than meets the eye. What's more, I'm starting to think they know exactly who we are ...'

'Hmmm. So I guess we wait it out and follow this coach back to wherever it's going next.'

'It's either that or try to catch the guy here, and I don't think that would be the best thing to do, given the surroundings.' Honoré looked pensive. 'Let's hold on and see where he leads us.'

HARBINGERS OF DARKNESS

They waited for about thirty minutes before they saw the hooded man return to the carriage. A young boy, obviously disturbed from his sleep by the ruffle of his hair and the manner in which his clothes had been hastily pulled on, attended to the horses, bringing them around the front of the old coach and attaching the harnesses. The man in the cloak grunted at the boy and clambered up onto the driver's seat. A moment later, he trundled out of the yard, driving the horses to a gentle trot.

Honoré and Emily emerged from their hiding place, keeping a cautious eye open for any other people who might still be milling around. Honoré guessed it must be about two-thirty in the morning. The night sky was still shrouded in syrupy fog and under-lit by the warm light of the sleeping city. Emily ran over to the horses' trough and dipped her arms in up to her elbows, scrubbing off the remaining blood as best she could. Honoré joined her and rubbed away the stain across her brow with a handful of water.

'Okay,' he told her, 'let's make sure we keep up with him.'

They slipped out into the street, checking in both directions, and then set off after the rattling sound of the carriage. Absently, Honoré wondered if the police had found the body of the dead man yet.

Thankfully, the driver of the carriage did not appear to be in any hurry, and it was not too difficult for Honoré and Emily to keep up, following the trundling horses at a pace that was half-walk and half-run. The few passers-by they saw as they made their way after the mysterious coach paid no heed to the two time-travellers, and Honoré supposed that they must have had their own reasons for being out on the streets at this time of night. Sometimes, it was better not to ask.

They continued for a good forty minutes or so, through the winding streets of the city, until the coach slipped down a narrow side street and out onto what appeared to be a circular road running around the edges of a small park. Honoré was unsure where they were, but some of the buildings looked strangely familiar. They waited out of sight by the edge of a wrought-iron railing that ran around the perimeter of the park, catching their breaths, watching for what the driver would do next. There was no-one else around, and all the other buildings in the vicinity were deathly quiet. There was a stillness in the air, a vague sense of foreboding, and both Honoré and Emily were silenced by the oppression, neither of them feeling the need to talk. It was almost as if they had entered a part of the city that was excluded from the normal humdrum of daily life; not even one house appeared to have a light in the window, and the only sound was the footfall of the horses and the creaking wheels of the old carriage as the driver pulled up to a large gate.

The horses came to a halt, their breath making great clouds of steam in the air around them. The hooded driver dismounted and made his way over to the gate. Emily strained to see. She thought she could just make out, on the other side of the gate, another, similarly dressed figure to whom who the driver was talking. Moments later, the driver was back in his seat and the carriage was trundling on through the gates, which were swung open with a loud grating sound by the other man – obviously a watchman or guard.

The coach disappeared into the interior of the park, following a winding path that was eventually swallowed by a large canopy of trees. Emily stood back and tried to take a measure of the railings.

'What do you reckon, Honoré, about five feet?'

'At the most. Here, I'll give you a lift over.' He reached down and supported her legs whilst she shimmied over the top of the railings, taking care not to snag herself on the sharp, originally ornamental points at the top.

. She dropped down easily on the other side.

'Okay, come on.'

Lechasseur followed suit, pulling himself up over the metal *fleurs-de-lis* and down onto the grass verge below.

'Where do you think we are?' he asked, glancing at Emily and trying to catch her attention. She was already making her way over to the trees, heading in the same direction as the carriage.

'I've no idea. Somewhere in the East End, I think. We can't be that far away from home.'

Honoré took one last look around, trying to work out why he had a such a strong sense of *déjà-vu*, before catching up with his companion and trying to get a sense of where the carriage might be. He was wary that they might be wandering into another carefully prepared trap.

Moments later, after making their way cautiously through the large boundary of trees, they came out on the other side; a huge space in the centre of the park. They could see the coach, parked up by the entrance to an imposing house, the two horses being freed of their harnesses and led away to rest. The driver was nowhere to be seen.

The house itself was a massive, ornate structure; a grand study of architecture. Its imposing Georgian entranceway, supported by two tall stone columns and surrounded by opulent detail, was flanked by a large wing to either side, two storeys tall, with magnificent windows that punctuated the entire length of the building. It was one of the most grandiose houses that Lechasseur had ever seen. Why he'd never seen it before, he couldn't think.

They continued to watch for a while, studying the house for any visible signs of movement. Around them, the fog started to gather and drift through the trees and over the rooftops. After a few minutes, the hooded driver reappeared at the entranceway with three colleagues, all adorned in similar attire, and they made their way down the steps to the carriage. Once again, the driver produced his staff from under his cloak, and rapped on the side of the wooden panel. Honoré and Emily were too far away to hear what was being said, but there was a lot of to-ing and fro-ing between the men, before one of them grasped hold of the carriage door and pulled it open.

The creature shot out like a bullet, knocking down one of the men and attempting to bolt away into the park. One of the others managed to grab hold of its left arm, and the driver stepped up and whipped it viciously around the head with his staff. Eventually, after a prolonged beating, the creature slumped limp on the gravel before his feet.

With all the commotion and the sudden blur of movement, Honoré had not been able to see clearly what it was the men had let loose from the carriage, but as they pulled it up onto its feet – its two feet – he was stunned to bear witness to such a horrible abomination.

It was a man, but a man who had been so horrifically mutilated and *altered* that he was now more monster than human being.

Emily, beside him, gasped in shock. 'Oh my God, it's Abraxas!'[2]

Lechasseur paused for a moment. 'It's not Abraxas, but it's something close.'

He looked more intently. The creature was a patchwork of body parts and mechanical limbs. Strange, rubber-like tubing ran from his throat to his chest, as if all his breathing was automated, pumped through his system by some wicked machine. His right arm was entirely mechanical, a strange, angular construct that looked as if it was intended to mirror not so much a human arm as a crude, bird-like talon. Patchwork leather criss-crossed his body, replacing large expanses of his own flesh, giving him a kind of dead, waxy look that suggested he was actually more an animated corpse than a living being. Just like Abraxas.

But it was his mouth that revealed the true horror of what this man had become. As he was poked and prodded in the direction of the building, the man cast his head back and howled into the night, a terrifying shriek of anguish and pain that made the hairs on the back of Honoré's arms stand on end and caused Emily to shiver as if she were icy cold.

And as his head was briefly silhouetted against the moonlight, both Honoré and Emily could see that the man actually had a second set of jaws; a set of razor-like metal teeth, embedded *inside* his own mouth, that thrust outwards as he howled. gnashing viciously at the air. It was as if he had no control over this horrendous additional body part, and that to keep it contained, he had to clamp his jaws shut and whimper

2 See *The Cabinet of Light.*

in defiance.

The driver continued to whip at the creature with his staff, until all five figures had disappeared inside, swallowed by the ornamental doorway.

Emily had tears welling up in the corners of her eyes. 'How could they do something like that? It's an abomination. Did you *see* anything, or get any idea where he was from?' She looked at Honoré over her shoulder.

'No. It all happened too fast. Besides, as horrific as it is, at least we now know what it is that's been tearing those poor people's throats out.' Their eyes met. 'I also think that whatever they've done to him is beyond the technology of this time period. There's something deeper and more worrying going on beneath all this. Something to do with time.'

Emily looked worried. 'I think you're right. But what do we do now? We still have no idea why they've been killing these people, or why the severed man led us to this time period.'

'We go take a look inside.' Honoré set out, moving around the edges of the line of trees, trying to see a different way in.

'What are you doing?' Emily joined him.

'A house of this size must have a servant's entrance. If we can find that, we could probably sneak in through the kitchen or something.'

'Good thinking. I'll take a look round this way.' She indicted the left wing. 'You take a look around there.'

They split up, heading in opposite directions, both looking for a way to get into the old house without being seen. For Honoré, the more worrying thought was what they might actually find inside.

Having both completed a half-circuit of the house, they met again around the rear of the building. Emily was the first to point out the door.

'Look, over there.' Honoré tried to see where she was pointing. 'No, *there*.' She jabbed her finger at the air. He tried to follow the line of it. Sure enough, there appeared to be a small wooden door at the back of the house, leading to, Honoré presumed, the servants' area.

'I think that's our best bet,' he agreed.

Emily rested her hand on his arm. 'What exactly are you hoping to find in there?'

'Some answers,' was Honoré's only response.

They checked quickly in both directions to make sure there was no-one else around in the grounds, then made a dash for the door, trying to tread as lightly as possible on the gravel to avoid detection.

Once they were both standing against the side of the house, Honoré tried the door.

'Be ready to run. The kitchen may be full of servants.'

The door cracked open with a loud creak. Holding his breath, Lechasseur stepped cautiously inside.

The room was deserted.

He beckoned to Emily to come through, and swung the door shut behind them. The room they were in had at one time been a kitchen, but now it appeared to be entirely abandoned, pots and pans laying about the place as if, one day, the staff had just upped and left and never returned.

Honoré made his way over to the table, where a chopping board lay covered in fibrous mould. The dust was thick and dry in his nostrils, and he had the sense that the room had not been used for a long time.

'What do you make of this?' he whispered to Emily, who was standing by the old range, trying to figure out what had been cooking in the pots.

'Looks like someone just walked out one day and never came back.'

'Just what I was thinking.'

'Except for the fact that the room is obviously used to get in and out of the house. Look at the marks on the floor over there. Not to mention the fact that the door was open.'

Honoré nodded. 'If the house isn't lived in, I wonder what they use it for?'

'I hate to think.' Emily placed one of the pans back on top of the stove. 'Let's move on before someone comes through.' She made her way to the door on the other side of the room. Little plumes of dust followed her in a trail as she walked across the floor. She turned to Lechasseur. 'Come on.'

He followed behind her, unsure. Things weren't working out the way he had expected them to.

Beyond the disused kitchen, a corridor fanned out in three directions. Straight ahead, Emily presumed, would lead them to the main entrance hall, so they decided to take a right and head towards the left wing of the house. There was no-one around in the corridor, but in contrast to the air of calm that pervaded outside the building, it was obvious that there was a great deal of activity going on in other parts of the house. Muffled noises and the occasional sound of voices could be heard coming from beneath them. The corridor itself was lined by blank white walls, with no sign of any of the paintings or plaques that Honoré would have expected to find in such an old, traditional manor house. The floor consisted of plain polished floorboards, and they had to move slowly to avoid making a noise and drawing attention to themselves.

Soon, the corridor terminated in a large hall. Again, the room seemed relatively abandoned, with no obvious evidence of recent occupation. An old, moth-eaten tapestry hung from the far wall, portraying a scene from the Bible based around The Last Supper. Honoré wondered if it had been left there as some sort of sick joke.

At the far end of the room, a small staircase led down to a lower level.

'What do you think? Down there or back the way we came?' Honoré was starting to feel a little edgy.

Emily looked back the way they had come. 'I say down. If we check it out down there and don't find anything, we can head back that way afterwards.'

Honoré thought he could still hear noises coming from beneath the hall, and urged caution. 'We could check upstairs first – make sure the way is clear?'

'Why don't we split up? You go upstairs, I'll head down. We can meet up again in a few minutes.'

'No. I think we should stick together. Let's head down and see what's going on. Just take it easy, and don't give the game away. I'm sure there are people down there.'

They made their way over to the staircase. From the makeshift way it had been put together, Honoré assumed it was a recent addition to the house. Many of the similar Georgian properties he had seen had large cellars, but they were usually accessed through the kitchen or from a doorway beneath the main stairs. To have a set of stairs in the main hall was unusual, to say the least.

He climbed down, stooping to try to make out what was at the bottom.

There was obviously something going on down there. A small tunnel had been carved out beneath the house, right through the very foundations; a long, thin passageway with a number of small doors leading off from it. The passageway was lit by a number of free-standing coal braziers. These cast a warm orange glow and enlivened the shadows, which danced around the walls like the players in a dark harlequinade.

Coming from the far end of the passageway, Honoré and Emily could hear a soft chanting, a repetitive set of words or sounds being sung over and over by a multitude of different voices. Honoré turned to Emily. 'I guess that's our Devil cult then.'

Emily looked a little shaken at the thought.

'You don't think it's Mestizer again, do you? Another group of Subterraneans summoning their god?'[3]

Lechasseur shook his head. 'I doubt it. I'll go take a look. You check out some of these rooms.' He strode down towards the end of the tunnel, and quickly disappeared around a slight bend. For a moment, Emily hesitated, unsure what to do. Then she went after him, jogging to try and catch up. She found him kneeling in an open doorway behind a brazier, trying to stay out of view. He glanced up at her, waving his hand sharply, telling her to get back. She pushed her back up against the wall and shuffled over to where he was crouching. From here, she could just about see what lay beyond.

It was a vast chamber, a huge underground cavern that had somehow been opened up and turned into a sort of temple or shrine. From the roughly-hewn passageway, a small set of steps led down into the cavernous space, a space that was filled, as far as Emily could see, with about fifty men and women, all dressed in dark black cloaks like the one worn by the driver of the carriage they had followed here.

On the far wall, a vast starscape had been painted in intricate detail;

3 See *The Tunnel at the End of the Light.*

a view of the night sky so realistic that Emily would have wondered if it were a window, had she not known that, outside, the fog had almost totally obscured the night sky. Of more concern, however, were the immense, horned effigies of the Devil that stood on either side of this starmap, staring out unblinkingly at the audience. A man was standing at the foot of one of these large statues, leading the others through the incantation. In his hand he held some sort of ancient book, and he was reading from it, pleading with some unseen entity to enrich the souls and enlighten the minds of the assembled throng. Emily couldn't quite hear everything he was saying, but the terminology sounded terribly familiar. He kept referring to 'pollutants of the time streams', and declaring that his people would 'cleanse the way'; saying that the 'time creature' was an invaluable gift, and would allow him to 'purge the forces of falsity forever'.

Emily caught Honoré's attention, but he simply shrugged. He didn't know what to make of it all. Together, they crept back up the passageway and away from the bizarre ceremony.

Once they'd rounded the bend, Honoré called a halt. 'Any idea what all that was about?'

Emily looked at him sternly 'No. You?'

'No. Except I'm now more sure than ever that these fanatics are responsible for the murders. But that doesn't explain where the tramp comes into it all, or how they're able to find all the time sensitive victims in the first place.'

'He said something about a "time creature"?'

'He said a whole load of stuff. I think most of it was just mumbo-jumbo. Cult stuff. Anyhow, let's check out what's in these rooms, while we've still got chance.'

They made their way over to one of the nearby doors. It was made of strong wood, with wrought iron hinges, and had been bolted shut from the outside. Honoré slid the bolt aside and cautiously opened the door.

The room was empty.

'Some sort of holding cell, I'd guess. Try the next one.'

Emily skipped over to the next door, eased the bolt out of its cradle and allowed the door to swing open. Then she fell back with a sudden scream, smashing into one of the braziers and upturning it, spilling burning coals all over the floor.

Honoré leapt towards her, knocking her clean out of the way and sending them both tumbling down the passageway, colliding with a second brazier and narrowly missing being engulfed by the flames.

They came to rest a few feet further down the tunnel. Honoré looked back to see what had startled Emily, and was nearly blinded by a sheet of intense white light that was flashing out of the room, searing his eyes. Almost transfixed, he managed to blink his eyes closed and look away. Baubles of white danced in front of his vision. Emily was on her feet.

'Come on! They're coming for us. They heard me scream. Come on!'

She pulled him to his feet and they span around, preparing to make a run for it.

The creature from the carriage was standing at the bottom of the stairs, staring at them.

Close up, the man looked even more horrific than Honoré had first thought. His skin was flayed and sore where it had been removed in great patches, and the leather that had been stitched in its place was tough and brittle. The mechanical talon where his right arm should have been twitched with nervous energy, and Lechasseur could tell that every movement inspired excruciating pain in its owner. The man opened his mouth as if he were trying to speak, but his terrible, scissor-like appendage shot out and gnashed at the air before him.

Emily screamed again.

Honoré could hear the cultists behind them, trying to fight their way through the flames that were now licking at the wooden doors and threatening to carry along the whole passageway. He eyed the creature in front of him. Even with the sound of the commotion behind him, Honoré could hear the laboured breath of the machine that had been implanted in the man's chest, and it reminded him terribly of Abraxas, the bizarre human-machine that he had encountered back in London so many months ago, when he first met Emily. He returned the man's gaze, looking into his eyes.

He saw nothing but pain and anguish. This man was not a killer, but a victim. Images flashed before his mind. He could see a young soldier, fighting in the trenches of the First World War, his rifle clutched tightly to his chest, panic rising within him as his officer gave the order to go over the top. He could see that same young man lying in a puddle of his own blood, his arm blown clear away by enemy fire.

He could see a field hospital, a doctor, a nurse, and a recruiting officer, looking for invalids who could continue to work for the causes of the war.

He could see a cramped, dark cell, an operating theatre and a series of horrific nightmares, in which a man in a leather smock cut away every last vestige of the man this soldier had once been.

Honoré hung his head.

When he looked back, the creature had stepped to one side to let them pass. Emily pulled him up the makeshift stairwell in a daze, bewilderment creasing her brow. But Honoré had seen the man for who he really was, and knew with certainty that the flames now engulfing the passageway were like a divine deliverance, bringing the relief of death to a man who had suffered through time and space at the hands of some terrible, evil force.

They scrambled into the hall at the top of the stairs and then out towards the main entrance of the building. As they rounded the corridor and flung themselves into the foyer, two hooded men came charging at them, blocking their way.

Lechasseur immediately launched into one of them, bowling him over. But the other caught him with a blow between the shoulder blades and he went down heavily, landing hard on the floor beside his first assailant.

Emily leapt into action. She spun on her heel, swinging her leg around in a high kick that caught the second man directly in the face and felled him like a dead weight. Just to be sure, she brought her foot down hard on his stomach to take the wind out of him.

Honoré was clambering to his feet, but all he managed to catch was a blur of motion before the other man was down on the ground again too, Emily's elbow smashing hard into his nose.

The two friends raced out of the house, running toward the fog-enshrouded trees and away to safety. Behind them, the house glowed red from the flames of the rapidly spreading fire. As they cleared the park and scrambled over the railings, Honoré was sure he caught the sound of screaming as the long-tortured soldier finally found his place of rest amongst the many, many dead.

THE MACHINATIONS OF INSANITY

Honoré and Emily fled into the dark night, unsure where they were going in the fog, but keen to put some distance between themselves and the cultists, who they knew, without a doubt, would be searching for them throughout the city.

After what seemed like an age, they stopped to rest and catch their breath.

They sat panting on a low wall, trying to make some sense out of what had happened.

'What the hell do you think that light was?' Honoré wheezed out through gritted teeth. His back was hurting badly from where he had been knocked to the floor by the cultist.

'I've no idea. Was it anything like the light you described in your dream?'

Honoré had almost forgotten about that. 'It was just like the light in the dream! Just before I see you coming towards me, that same light is there, blinding me!'

'And what about that horrible creature? Why do you think it let us past?'

Honoré smiled. 'You're right, it was horrible. But the man underneath was very human, and in very real pain. He was a soldier – just like Abraxas – who had been tortured and controlled, modified into that horrific *thing*. Not only that, he was from a different time zone entirely. There's something going on here that I don't yet understand.'

'It's as if this time period is some sort of convergence point, a nexus of some kind.'

'That's exactly it. All these disparate threads coming together. Which probably means that the other points in time in which the tramp is active are the same.'

'It would make sense.'

They sat there for a while, mustering strength. After a time, Emily jumped down from the wall and paced backwards and forwards in front of Honoré.

'Look,' she said, resolutely, 'we can talk this over in the morning. Let's go and find somewhere to get some proper rest.'

'I don't think the B&B will be safe anymore.'

'We'll find somewhere else then. If we don't get some sleep soon, we'll be no good tomorrow. Come on.'

She started off down the road. Lechasseur jumped down and caught her up. 'What did you make of those Devil statues?'

'I told you – let's talk about it in the morning.'

'Emily …'

She sighed. 'There has to be some sort of connection to my past. Every time I see those images, I just freeze. They keep popping up in my dreams, too; I can't sleep without seeing images of the Devil everywhere I look.' She looked exasperated, tired and a little scared.

Honoré slipped his arm around her shoulders. 'Okay, let's talk it over in the morning.'

They made their way across the city, wandering aimlessly, looking for somewhere to get some rest. They were both exhausted, drained after the adrenaline rush of the night's events, and desperately in need of sleep. Just as they were about to stop for another quick rest, Honoré realised he knew where they were.

'Look! That's the old church at the back of Spitalfields market.' He pointed it out. The church tower stood fully intact, a round clock-face proud on its frontage. It was a stark contrast to the bombed-out mess of a building that still stood in the marketplace in 1950.

The moonlight was finally starting to wane as the sun was rising in the East and burning away great clumps of the clinging fog. Through the haze, Honoré could just make out the graveyard that ran around the grounds of the old church.

'We've got to check this out.' He led Emily across the street and toward the imposing building. As they drew nearer, the sound of voices could be heard from further into the graveyard, and every now and then, the sound of a spade shuffling soil around. Honoré and Emily peered over the wall, searching out the source of the noise.

Two men were standing beneath the branches of a large tree, digging. It looked, from where Lechasseur was standing, as if they were opening up a recently interred grave.

Emily looked at him quizzically. 'What do you think they're up to?'

Honoré shrugged. 'Let's find out.' He swung his leg up over the wall and strode towards the two diggers, fully expecting them to drop their spades and run. Grave robbers were a common curse of the Victorian church yards, he recalled, and the penalties were harsh.

When one of the men saw him coming, he cried out: 'Christ, Jeffries, look!'

The other man turned and looked at Lechasseur. 'In the name of God!' He dropped his spade into the hole before him.

Honoré looked them over. He could hear Emily clambering over the wall behind him. 'What's going on?'

'Here, Jeffries, I can't believe it.'

Jeffries nodded.

Honoré gave an exasperated snort. 'Can't believe what?'

The first man piped up again. 'Can't believe that you actually showed up, is what! This nobleman, right, comes to us three weeks ago and gives us fifty pounds *apiece* to dig up this 'ere grave, on this day, at this exact time. Says a big black man and a woman will show up just before we lift the coffin out of the ground.'

'And ...'

'And we're just about to lift the coffin out o' the ground.'

The two men cleared their tools out of the way and reached into the grave, grasping at the ropes that had been used to lower the coffin into the ground when it was first prepared. Honoré leaned over and looked at the name on the tombstone. The legend read:

Barnaby Tewkes.
1892.
He Lives On.

He nearly laughed out loud.

The two men managed to slide the coffin out onto the firm ground by the side of the hole. The coffin looked relatively new, and they brushed the soil away easily with their hands.

'You want us to open it then, sir?'

Emily, who was still trying to understand what was going on, looked at Lechasseur in dismay. 'What the …?'

He cut her off. 'Yeah, go ahead and open it up.'

Emily looked away in disgust.

Jeffries produced a crowbar and set to work levering the coffin lid away from the base. A moment later, and with a hideous screeching sound, the retaining nails came free, and the two men together lifted the lid away with a pained look on their faces.

There was a moment of silence as they all looked at each other, no-one wishing to be the first to peer into the coffin. Then the corpse sat up straight with a sudden jerk.

Emily let out a shriek, and Honoré instinctively stepped towards her.

One of the men started to say something reassuring. 'I seen that before, sir, when you open a coffin up …' His voice trailed off when he realised that the corpse was actually giggling to itself uncontrollably.

Emily let out another shriek.

But Honoré was already lost in the swirling, colliding time zones and the wretched stumps of severed time that circled this giggling corpse like a tempestuous aura. He clutched hold of Emily, and they disappeared in a brief, crackling blue electrical haze.

PART THREE: THE IMPOSITION OF VIRTUE

FADED REVELATIONS

Daylight. The sun beating down on his face like a wash of golden water, a bronze dream. Lechasseur rolled onto his side and peered into the light.

He was in a field.

Beside him, Emily lay on the grass, her hair a tangle of loose strands, her dress a crumpled mess of faux Victorian finery. His mind was still reeling from the step through time. He rolled onto his back. The sky was a clear blue, with white, fluffy candy-floss clouds scudding across his view. He had no idea what year it was.

He sat up. It felt like he'd left his head on the floor. His vision swam for a moment, before settling down to a steady spin. He tried to blink it away.

There was no-one else around, as far as he could see. He guessed they were in a farmer's field, or the countryside; in the distance, he could see some sheep grazing on the grass in the sunshine.

He looked down at Emily.

She was still unconscious.

He climbed onto his knees and shuffled over towards her.

He thought she looked angelic lying there, with her eyes closed and her hair spread around her head. He reached down and gently smoothed a stray strand from her face. The strange circumstances that had brought them together had changed his life. And had brought him

Emily. They were not lovers, were not romantically linked, but he knew he would do anything, go anywhere for Emily.

Emily didn't appear to be hurt, and he assumed, for the moment, that the chain of events that had landed them here had simply been too much for her and she needed to rest. Given that there didn't seem to be anyone around to bother them, he rolled over onto his back and allowed himself to close his own eyes for a few minutes too. He needed to get some energy back before he went looking for Barnaby Tewkes.

A little while later, Honoré was woken by the sound of Emily saying his name. He opened his eyelids slowly. She was kneeling over him, her hand gently prodding his shoulder. He was still lying in the field, but he figured a couple of hours must have passed since he'd first woken, as he felt considerably more refreshed. He looked up at Emily, who continued to prod him nervously.

'Honoré. Wake up. There's someone coming.'

He sat up, glancing around to either side. In the distance, he could make out the shape of a man climbing the ridge towards them, a shotgun cocked over one arm.

He blinked his eyes blearily, trying to wake himself up.

Emily was trying to get his attention again. 'Are you okay, Honoré?'

'Fine. Are you?'

'Yes.'

'Let's get out of here, then.' They both climbed to their feet and dusted themselves down. The farmer, who was getting nearer now, hadn't paid them even the slightest bit of attention.

They scanned the horizon, and, after deciding which direction to take, began to make their way towards what they thought looked like a small village in the distance, about a mile or so away. Smoke was winding its way out of a distant chimney, curling in the gentle breeze.

Honoré had a dry, sticky mouth and needed something to drink.

The farmer, by this time, was only about twenty feet away. He continued to ignore the two strangers, not even bothering to cast them a glance. Emily smiled at Honoré. 'Perhaps he's embarrassed?'

'Why?'

'He's just seen a man and a woman get up out of his field and dust themselves down.'

'Ah, I see what you mean. Let's leave him to his embarrassment. We should be able to make it to that village in about half an hour or so. I could do with something to drink.'

They set out, strolling in the mid-morning sunshine. The events of just a few hours earlier seemed like days ago to Lechasseur, and he decided to try and enjoy the time he had before he arrived at the village, where he presumed he would find the elusive Mr Barnaby Tewkes. He hoped that, in this time period – whenever that was – he would be able to get a few answers.

They arrived at the outskirts of the village after about forty minutes of walking. Emily was hot and bothered in her long Victorian dress, and Honoré had shed his black leather coat and was carrying it folded over one arm.

People were milling around, going about their daily business. Nearby, a woman was feeding some ducks with her little boy, and further down the road, a man was nailing a sign on the front of his house. It read: *Beware of the Dog.*

Honoré laughed at the sheer sugariness of it all; it was like a fairytale English village, replete with all the stereotypical villagers and picture-postcard buildings.

They strode into the village square, hoping not to draw too much attention in their out-of-place clothes.

No-one looked.

Not a single soul even turned a head to catch a glimpse of the newcomers. Honoré, oddly disturbed, stopped by the well in the centre of the village square. A woman was filling a bucket, drawing on the rope to bring her pail back up to the surface. He approached her slowly.

'Excuse me, can you tell us the name of this village?'

No response. Again, the woman didn't even look up from her work, but just continued drawing the bucket up the well shaft as if nobody had spoken.

Emily stepped towards her. 'Excuse me, miss, we're a little lost and looking for somewhere to rest?'

Still the woman continued to ignore them. Lechasseur caught Emily's eye with a wary glance. 'Any ideas?'

'Let's try talking to someone else.'

She approached one of a group of boys playing with a hoop against the side of a nearby house. 'Hello there. We're new around here and looking for somewhere to stay. Could you possibly give us some directions?'

The boy continued to bang his hoop against the wall, oblivious to their presence. Emily looked back at Honoré.

A bird crowed overhead.

They drifted towards each other across the village square. The villagers continued to bustle around them, carrying on with their normal routines.

'What do you make of all this?' Honoré looked a little shell-shocked, as if he had just walked out of one nightmare and straight into another.

'It's as if we don't exist. It's not like they're purposely ignoring us. There's no little glance out the corner of the eye or surreptitious whisper that some newcomers have arrived. They simply don't know we exist.'

'Do you think the jump through time went wrong? Could we be stuck here, where no one can see or hear us?'

'I don't know, Honoré, I really don't. I hope not.'

'Let's try the pub. At least we may be able to get something to drink in there.'

They made their way toward the large inn that sat on one side of the village square, just next to a cricket pitch and opposite a small church. Lechasseur walked around the front to take a look. The sign showed an old, faded picture of a black and white sow, and the legend below it read: *The Old Dun Cow*. A couple of people were sitting outside, having a drink. They ignored Lechasseur as he walked by their table.

He found Emily around the back of the building, looking up at the blue sky.

'It's nice to be away from all that Devil stuff, Honoré, even if we are lost in a nameless village where no-one will even acknowledge our existence.'

Honoré smiled. 'I know exactly what you mean.' He turned his head toward the building. 'The pub looks to be okay. Same story, though. The two men around the front wouldn't acknowledge I was there.'

'Let's try inside.'

They ducked their heads under the low beam that hung above the doorway and slipped into the darkness inside.

The building was obviously hundreds of years old; the upper storey leaned outwards as if it were made from melted wax. Inside, the old wooden beams ran across the ceiling space in a criss-cross that reminded Emily of a game of noughts and crosses. The bar was propped in one corner like an afterthought, a rude addition to the magnificence of the eccentric old building.

A few people were sitting at tables, enjoying a drink with their friends. Two men were sitting at the bar, chatting with the barman, a dark, stocky man with a long beard and a large, rotund belly.

Honoré made his way over to the bar and tried to get the barman's attention.

'Yes, what can I get you?' the man replied, smiling pleasantly.

Honoré jumped in surprise, but quickly composed himself. 'Er, just two glasses of water, please.'

'Coming right up.'

The man turned away and began preparing their drinks. As Emily joined him at the bar, Honoré tried to catch the attention of the two men sitting on bar stools beside him, but they were either lost in their own conversation or, like the people outside, simply unable to see him. A moment later, the barman returned with two pints of bitter, which he placed on the bar in front of Honoré.

'No, I asked for two glasses of water, please.'

'Yes, what can I get you?' The man smiled at him in a cheery fashion, and Honoré let out a long groan. The man turned back to his two friends at the bar and stroked his beard absently.

'I think we're fighting a losing battle here.' He turned to Emily. 'Shall we see if we can find ourselves a base somewhere? Somewhere to have a wash and find some clothes? You've still got splashes of blood on the front of your dress.'

'Good idea. It doesn't look like we're going to get any answers here.'

They left their pints of ale on the bar and made their way back out into the bright daylight.

For another hour they walked around the village, trying to provoke responses from the villagers. Lechasseur even attempted to take hold of one of them physically, but the man just seemed to glaze over and lose consciousness until Lechasseur let him go, at which point he carried on his way as if nothing had happened. Emily was finding it more than a little spooky, and Honoré seemed even more on edge than he had the previous night. It was as if they had suddenly been isolated from normality, shut out from the safety of the real world, and, to Honoré, that was even more terrifying than any cultist, or even any Devil, he might have to face.

After a while, they decided to take a look inside a small bed-and-breakfast they had noticed when they had first entered the village. They made their way back there, passing across the village square where the woman was still drawing water from the well and the children were still banging their hoop up against the wall with gleeful cheers. There was an eerie sort of consistency to it all, like everything was just carrying on as normal and had been that way for years.

Soon enough, they managed to track down the lodging house. It was a small, detached cottage, out of the way of the main road that ran idly through the village. The roof was a dark grey thatch that reminded Honoré of nothing so much as an old woman's hair, all dry and crisp. It made him think momentarily of Mrs Bag-of-Bones, his landlady back in 1950. She was probably happily engaged in making herself a cup of tea, or sitting alone in her kitchen, the world slowly passing her by in a predictable, linear fashion.

Honoré led the way up the cobbled path, ducking his head under a rose arch that had overgrown slightly to create a kind of thorny obstacle along the way.

There was a sign on the door that said *Rooms Available*, so Emily tried the handle, and when it opened, stepped inside. In the hallway, an old lady was polishing a mirror, a lurid blue pinafore tied around her waist and a pair of small spectacles perched neatly on the end of her nose. Emily approached her cautiously, fully expecting her not to respond. When she didn't, it was almost a relief.

Emily was just about to turn around and suggest to Honoré that they go and find a room, when a voice from behind her said, 'Don't mind old Mrs Wickham, she never did have very good hearing, even when she was at her best.'

Both Honoré and Emily span around in surprise.

A man was standing behind them, dressed in a smart black suit and leaning casually against the doorframe. He was drinking tea from a small china cup.

He raised an eyebrow, obviously enjoying their surprise. 'Tea?'

The man stepped back into the living room to allow them space to enter. They both shuffled inside, cautious of what this stranger might do and how he might react to their presence. Honoré took a seat in an old armchair by the fireplace, and Emily perched on a stool in the corner, her back to the wall, as if she were scared someone else may try to catch her out from behind. She looked expectantly at Honoré, as if she was waiting for him to say something.

The man disappeared into another room for a moment and returned with two cups. A teapot was sitting on a small table in the centre of the room. He set the cups down on it and regarded the two friends keenly.

'I have the pleasure, do I not, of addressing Miss Emily Blandish …' he offered a bow in her direction, '… and Mr Honoré Lechasseur.'

He held out his hand to Honoré, who pointedly ignored it.

'You have us at a disadvantage, sir.'

The man smiled. 'Oh, excuse my manners. I am the man you've been looking for. I am Barnaby Tewkes.'

Honoré tried to get a measure of the man. It was clear, now that he looked closely, that this was the same person they had seen in both 1950 and 1892 – his severed time-snake still whipped around him like a wild, thrashing thing. But he was more together here, more *sane* than they had seen him before. He was clean-shaven, for a start, and dressed in clothes appropriate to the era. But it was more than that. He seemed to have a flash of intelligence about him, a depth that had been lacking in his previous incarnations. Yet there was still an air of danger about him, a frisson that put Honoré on edge. He shifted uncomfortably in the chair.

Barnaby poured them each a cup of tea, then passed the cups out, playing the role of the genial host. He settled himself in a chair opposite Lechasseur. In the hallway, Mrs Wickham continued to clean the telephone stand with her duster, working away at the cracks to ensure everything would be clean for her perpetually non-existent guests.

'What's the matter with them?' Honoré indicated the old lady with a nod of his head, as he took a sip of his tea.

'All in good time, all in good time. I believe we should start at the beginning, as we have much to discuss. First, let's drink our tea.' Barnaby took a sip from his cup, revelling in the theatre of his own performance. He glanced at Emily. 'Miss Blandish, I believe we've met before?'

Emily nearly jumped out of her skin. 'We have?' She glanced at Lechasseur, but he was staring intently at Barnaby, waiting to hear more. 'Where? *When?*'

'You don't remember? Interesting. I too have been having some difficulty with my memory of late. Comes from being dead, and all that.' He shrugged, as if his comments were of little importance.

'Dead?' Lechasseur sat forward.

'Ah, I believe we're getting ahead of ourselves again, Mr Lechasseur.' He drawled Honoré's name elaborately. 'As for Miss Blandish …' He turned his head. 'I apologise, I can help you no further.' He brandished his teacup as if it signified his intentions towards her. 'I recall only that we have met, at some point in a future time period, but my memory of late has been shot to pieces – unravelled, you might say – and I can provide no further details. In truth, I was hoping you might be able to fill in some of the blanks.'

'I'm suffering from *amnesia.*' Emily spat the word angrily. 'I have memories reaching back only a few months, and no real notion of where I came from or how I got to where I am.'

'How truly dreadful. You have my sympathies, Miss Blandish, as well as my empathy.' Barnaby placed his cup down gently on the mantelpiece. 'Mustn't let Mrs Wickham see that, tsk, tsk.' He shook his head at himself and smiled.

Emily glanced at Honoré, who raised a questioning eyebrow.

'To answer your question, my dear Honoré, the people of this village are all enthralled by an alien entity from outside linear time. This entity has found a way to interfere with the minds of the townsfolk and is bending their will towards some unknown end. Effectively, they are walking around in a trance, and they are all entirely devoted to this entity as if it were some divine being from another realm; an angel or some such.'

Honoré coughed loudly as his tea went down the wrong way. He spluttered for a response, but wasn't quick enough before the other man continued.

'I believe you have encountered this entity already, locked in an underground cell in the bowels of the old house that serves as the meeting place of the Cabal of the Horned Beast.'

Honoré nodded slowly. 'That blinding light ...'

Barnaby reached into his jacket pocket and withdrew a small card, which he flicked onto the table with a flourish. Honoré picked it up. It was a copy of the same Tarot card that they had found at the various murder scenes during their time in Victorian London. He looked back at Barnaby, who was smiling at him, confident he had their attention.

'You see, I myself was a traveller, not unlike the two of you. With a companion, I was able to traverse the time streams, moving from period to period, sometimes involving myself in various goings-on and sometimes hiding away to seek respite from my daily existence. Now, however, I find myself trapped in numerous disparate time zones, with no ability to remove myself, and the prospect of a gradually encroaching termination at the ravages of insanity and memory loss. I believe I have encountered you in 1950, and in 1892, and now, here in 1921. I'm not sure of the order of these encounters, though.' His voice dropped to a mutter. 'Though this can't be the first, as I already know your names ...'

Honoré looked a little incredulous.

'Why do you think this has happened to you?' Emily leaned forward towards Barnaby, attempting to draw him out.

'I believe I was murdered at some point in the future, and all that's left of me now is a shadow, a flash-image of my former self, trapped in the time zones I visited before I died. How long these states will last, I don't know, but I do feel my memories fading away, like tiny bubbles bursting, and I believe it will not be too long before I entirely lose my mind.'

Emily nodded, obviously concerned.

Honoré couldn't help conjuring up the image of the gibbering man sitting in his own coffin, after having had himself buried alive for three weeks, only to be disinterred again later, according to a premonition. He considered the insanity to be nearer than Barnaby could ever begin to imagine.

'How do you know all this? And how did you know our names and where to find us, or when we would show up at the graveyard in 1892?' Honoré tried to catch Barnaby's eye.

'I've been travelling for a long time, and you learn to be able to sense people out, to *know* instinctively when someone shares that pulsating, binding connection to time. That's a part of it, certainly; but I also feel our stories are more intertwined than that, more vital. How and why, or even when, I truly cannot say.' Barnaby banged the heel of his hand against the side of his head, as if indicating his frustration at his failing mind.

Honoré tried to take in what he had said.

It was Emily's turn to chip in. 'Can you tell us more about the cult … the … The Cabal of the Horned Beast?'

Barnaby cast her a suspicious look – just a momentary glance out of the corner of his eye, but enough to make Lechasseur feel uneasy again - before he continued.

'Originally, the Cabal was just another, run-of-the-mill Victorian devil cult. A bunch of immature occultists with a penchant for drug abuse and fornication. They had no real philosophy or sense of spirituality behind their silly games; it was more an excuse to indulge in debauchery and depravity at the expense of others. Somewhere along the line, though, they were infiltrated by travellers from the future, who introduced their own agenda and began making use of the Cabal as a front for their own, more sinister activities in that time period.'

'So, what is that agenda?' Honoré was starting to see connections in what Barnaby was saying. *Travellers from the future …*

'The cult is obsessed with the "purity" of the time streams. They see time travel as a kind of pollution; a muddying of the waters. This faction believe that they are protecting time by eliminating all of the time sensitive people from history. Essentially, they are working their way through the past, murdering anyone who shows even a glimmer of sensitivity to the wider timeframes around them. The Cabal are their right arm in the nineteenth century, and as such, have been provided with information and technologies well beyond their era's own means.'

Honoré was shaking his head. 'Like the soldier from the First World War who had been turned into that horrible … beast.'

'Indeed. And, more significantly, the time entity they are hosting in their underground lair.' Barnaby gave a small cough and retrieved his teacup from the mantelpiece, taking another swig.

Emily leaned forward again, intent now on drawing as much out of Tewkes as she could. 'So you're saying that the entity that has control of all the people in this village is the same thing we encountered underground in 1892 – all that intense light – and that it was actually helping the cultists to locate and murder all those time sensitive people?'

Barnaby nodded. 'That's exactly what I'm saying.'

Once again, Honoré and Emily exchanged glances. Things were starting to make a little more sense.

'What about in 1950?' Honoré was fired up now, feeling as if they were drawing near to understanding what was actually going on. 'Is the entity around in 1950?'

'I … don't know. Either I have yet to locate it, or else my mind in that time period has atrophied to the extent that I have no memories of what has transpired.' He sat back, obviously tired.

'So tell us more about yourself,' said Emily. 'Who do you think was responsible for your death? And how far into the future are we talking – years, decades, centuries?' Emily was prodding for information again, and Lechasseur could see that it was making Barnaby very uncomfortable.

'I really have no answers for you, Miss Blandish. All that I recall is that I was working to try to discover the intentions of the entity, its motives for invading human time periods. My suspicions led me to believe that my death must have something to do with the time-cult from the future, the people responsible for bringing the entity here and murdering all those time sensitives you saw. They must have active groups in other time periods, as well as in the nineteenth century.' He mopped at his brow with a handkerchief he produced from his jacket pocket. 'Somewhere along the way, I seem to have lost my companion; whether she is also lost in a different time period, or even dead, I cannot say.'

'Do you think that Emily could be in the same position as you? Killed in the future, and existing only as a kind of living memory in the time periods she's visited?' Honoré had asked the question that Emily herself had been too scared to voice.

'I couldn't say.'

Emily looked at Honoré with wide, worried eyes.

For some time, the three of them sat around in the old cottage talking, discussing the future and the past, Emily and Lechasseur slowly building up a more complete picture of what they had become involved in. Barnaby, Honoré grew increasingly convinced, was already on the verge of insanity, and appeared to have lost a great deal of his memory. His, though, had been a gradual decline, a slow dying of the mind, whereas Emily's memory loss had seemingly occurred in one fell swoop, like a blackboard being wiped clean, a flower renewed. The same contrast was apparent in their respective time-snakes. Barnaby's was a severed, wretched stump of colliding time. Emily's, on the other hand, was entirely non-existent. Honoré wondered if that might have had something to do with the man who had introduced him to his new life all those many months ago.[4] Had *he* also played a part in Emily's situation?

Nevertheless, there remained Emily's extreme reaction to the Devil-cult and the symbols of their worship; a fact that made Honoré suspicious that they might indeed have had some responsibility for her current state of mind and her initial appearance in 1949. From the look on her face during their conversation with Barnaby, he could tell

4 See *The Cabinet of Light.*

that she was thinking the same thing.

After a time, Barnaby stood. 'I'll make us a fresh pot of tea.'

Lechasseur handed him his cup and saucer. 'And then what?'

Barnaby's eyes flashed with excitement. 'Then we storm the stronghold of the entity and attempt to free the people of the village from its thrall!' He looked at them both in turn. 'What say you?'

Emily nodded slowly, and looked to Honoré for guidance. 'Honoré, what do you think?'

'I think we should talk it over whilst Barnaby makes that second pot of tea.'

Barnaby smiled and walked out of the room, the china jangling in his hands as he danced around Mrs Wickham, who was still polishing earnestly in the hallway.

Emily came to sit beside Honoré, perching on the arm of his chair. 'Well?'

'Well, what do we know about this guy? How do we know we can trust him?'

'We don't.' Emily looked suddenly serious. 'But everything he's told us makes sense to me. The picture is beginning to come together. The entity in the basement of that building, the Devil-cult, the people of this village who are locked out of reality. He's even explained why his time-snake is all broken and severed. All those murders, Honoré – shouldn't we try to do something to help?'

'He may not be able to tell you any more about your own past – or future – you know. Just don't pin any hopes on him. He could be dangerous; he's already losing his mind. Remember what he was like back in the nineteenth century. What if it's all a pack of lies, a trap?'

'Do you honestly believe that, Honoré? Do you honestly believe that he's just sat there and made all that up?'

Lechasseur met her gaze, and sighed. 'No, I don't. But what I do know is that he's now asking us to run headlong into danger alongside him, and we've only known him for an hour or two.'

'But Honoré, this is what it's all been about! The dreams, the murders, the skipping through time, running around London in the dark and the rain. If we can put a stop to it, here, now, we can go home again knowing that everything is going to be okay.'

'Until the next time.' Honoré shrugged and smiled. 'Okay, we'll give him the benefit of the doubt.'

'Marvellous to hear it!' Barnaby appeared in the doorway, brandishing a fresh pot of tea. 'Let's bolster ourselves with this fresh infusion, then we can get moving. I'm sure Mrs Wickham would be delighted.'

Emily laughed at the sheer absurdity of it all, and reached for the jug of milk on the table.

THE HOUSE OF ANGELS

The ridge overlooking the old manor house was a good half a mile from the edge of the village. The three travellers had walked there together, Barnaby telling the other two of his plans as they strolled in the waning afternoon sunlight. The sky was still bright with a hazy, golden warmth, but the sun had begun to slip in the sky, and Honoré suspected that it would be dark before another two hours had passed. After dark was always a far better time to stage an ambush or a raid. They were crouched together on the edge of the low ridge – a kind of ruffle of earth that ran around one side of the village like a geological shelf – looking down on the large manor house in which Barnaby believed the entity to have taken up residence.

The house itself was a massive Tudor mansion; a stone-built decoration on the landscape, with twirling brick chimney stacks and beautiful, bold window frames. A large wing to one side of the property had been erected by felling two great oaks together and building a fretwork of beams and panels around them, and the effect was to make the entire structure seem as if it had sprouted from the ground like some sort of naturally orchestrated phenomenon.

A warm breeze was blowing in from the east, and Emily raised her face towards it, allowing the air to wash over her. 'It's such a lovely place, surrounded by fields and trees. Very different from London.'

Honoré nodded. 'True. But it feels a bit … *parochial.* I miss the buzz of the city when I'm not there.'

Emily laughed. 'Honoré Lechasseur: Metropolitan Man. I bet this place would seem a whole lot livelier if the people actually knew we were here.'

The three of them had passed through the square again on their way out of the village, and again had been met with not so much as a look. It was as if all of the residents were trapped in a perpetual loop, a cycle of activity from which they could not break free. Barnaby believed that to be a symptom of their servitude to the entity, but Honoré wasn't so sure; he couldn't see what use the people would be to the time creature if they were trapped in a permanent state of flux. He wondered if there was more to it than that. Maybe they had been wrapped in their tiny stasis bubbles to protect them from something?.

The activity around the manor house was minimal. A couple of gardeners were tending to the flowerbeds around the very edges of the estate, but were of little real concern. More worrying were the two burly men standing guard directly outside the front entrance.

'I'll wager there are two other chaps like that around the back.' Barnaby shifted his jacket on his shoulders. He'd stripped off his tie before leaving Mrs Wickham's cottage in the village.

Honoré felt that the whole setup seemed terribly familiar. 'Well, if it's anything like the last big house we broke into, most of the activity will be centred around one point, a great hall or something. Maybe even underground again.'

'Oh, I don't doubt it, my friend.' Barnaby patted him lightly on the arm. 'But hopefully less dangerous, hmm? I don't believe the time-cult are directly involved in the operations here; and if they are, they're focused on something entirely different. There have certainly been no dead bodies turning up in Middleton Bassett of late.'

Emily smiled. At least that was something.

Honoré got to his feet. 'Okay, I'm going to skirt around the grounds and try to see a way in, or at least try to get a better idea about what's going on inside. I vote we don't make a move for a couple of hours anyway, until the light is on our side.'

'Agreed. We'll stay here and keep a look out.' Barnaby nodded at Emily. 'I'm sure Miss Blandish will keep me on my toes.'

Honoré scrambled away down the incline towards some bramble bushes on the ridge, in an attempt to gain some cover. A waist-high, dry-stone wall ran around the perimeter of the grounds. Once he was behind it, Honoré kept low and shuffled along, until Emily couldn't seem him anymore for the undergrowth.

After a few moments had passed, and she was sure they were alone, Emily turned to Barnaby. 'Can you tell me anything more about the future? I need to know what happened to me, where I came from, what my life was in the time before I met Honoré. It terrifies me that I have no concept of where I came from.'

Barnaby smiled. 'My dear, you know how it is. My mind is in tatters – I have no memory of the future, and very little of the past. I don't expect to live very much longer, and I want to try to achieve something with what dwindling time I have left. All I know is that this cult, these time-travellers from the distant future, are becoming more and more active, more and more dangerous with every day that goes by, and that the entity they have summoned here needs to be destroyed or banished as quickly as possible, before more of us are lost forever.'

Emily was practically shaking at the thought of it. She couldn't help wondering if the entity they were about to face had played a detrimental part in her own existence. 'Something happened to me, something terrible, in the time before I found myself in 1949, and I *know* it has something to do with the Cabal. The things I saw, the symbols they were carrying, they *meant* something to me, and they terrified me. But for what reasons, I can't remember.'

Barnaby was staring off into the distance. 'Sometimes ...' he murmured. 'Sometimes ... I get flashes, as if my mind is trying to show me why it won't let me remember. Screams ... and blood ... always blood ...' He shuddered and blinked, coming back to the present and to Emily. 'We must put it out of mind,' he continued. 'We have a task at hand, and when your friend returns, we'll know what we have to do to achieve our aims. I can only assure you that I do know how you feel. My mind is slowly disintegrating, reeling and reeling, and all my attempts to keep it together are failing. It's as if I'm trying to catch spilling water with my bare hands.'

Emily looked away from Barnaby and the old house, allowing the breeze to ruffle her hair about her face. The wind reminded her, momentarily, of the tides of time, and she thought of herself and Honoré, swimming against them, pushing their way through against the force of the flow. Sometimes – and particularly since meeting Barnaby – she had wondered if it would be better to take up residence in one time period and create a normal, stable life. But she was acutely aware of how deeply the need to travel was set down in her bones, and of how, if she let it, her memory loss would eat away at her until she ended up in the same state as the dying traveller who sat on the ridge beside her.

That was too much to give away.

They waited for darkness to come, enjoying the silence of the warm evening and the reassurance of each other's company as the tension and anxiety of what they were about to do hung above them like a dreaded weight, waiting to fall.

THE SHROUD OF LIGHT

After about an hour and a half, Emily was startled by the sudden reappearance of Honoré behind her. He had come up and around the ridge from the other direction, completely circling the old house in an effort to identify the best way in. She hadn't seen him approaching in the growing darkness.

Honoré's shoes made light scuffing sounds on the grass as he walked towards them.

'Well, what did you find?' Barnaby was anxious to proceed. He kept fiddling nervously with his fingers, as if trying to steady a nervous twitch.

'The back way is barricaded, and the window frames are all stone – we could break the glass, but we wouldn't be able to get through the gaps in the stonework. I think we're going to have to go through the goons at the front.'

Barnaby looked pained. 'Really? No other way in?'

'I can't see one. Let's hope they're as oblivious to our presence as the people in the village.'

Emily shook her head. 'Somehow, I doubt that very much.'

They clambered up and began making their way down the incline in the shadowy light, making use of the scrub and bushes as cover. The house was cast thoroughly in darkness, and the two guards had stepped back into the doorway itself, retreating from the growing chill and the night breeze that had now transformed itself into a cold wind. Barnaby whispered over his shoulder to Lechasseur as they found the dry-stone wall and ducked down behind it for a moment to decide how to tackle the two men. 'Do you think there's anyone else inside? It seems awfully dark.'

'I couldn't tell from walking around the place, but it seemed quiet. The only people I saw were the two guys on the front. We may find we get inside and there's no one else around.'

Barnaby winked at Emily, who was looking nervously over Honoré's shoulder. 'Oh, I think we'll find what we're looking for inside. I've been doing this sort of thing for far too long to get it wrong this time.'

Honoré shrugged noncommittally. 'Okay, so you take the one on the left, I'll take the one on the right?' He nodded towards the other man.

Barnaby looked a little put out. 'Well, I must say it's not my usual type of thing, but needs must.'

They counted to three and leapt over the short wall, running towards the entrance, their feet churning up the gravel of the driveway. As predicted, the two men came hurtling out of the doorway to meet the on-comers, inquisitive looks turning to surprise at the sight of a large black man in a leather trench coat and a slight man in a black suit hurtling towards them. They readied themselves in preparation for defence.

Suddenly, just as the four men were about to come together in a clash of fists and bodies, the guard on the left dropped to the ground, followed in quick succession by the guard on the right. Lechasseur nearly went bowling over the prone form of his target, and had to catch himself so as not to lose his footing.

A moment later, when he had righted himself, he looked up to see what had happened. Emily was standing there in front of him, her shoe in her hand, the two unconscious men lying by her feet. Barnaby had started to chuckle loudly and was slowly clapping his hands in approval. Honoré looked at her quizzically.

'How about I take the one on the left *and* the one on the right?' She smiled, before replacing her shoe and turning about towards the entrance to the house. 'Now, do we need a key or something?'

Honoré laughed and shuffled up beside her. 'That's twice you've done that. Thanks.' He smiled, putting a hand on her arm before edging his way over towards the doorway.

The door was open where the two men had been standing in the entrance, sheltering from the night wind. Honoré stepped into the hallway, looking around. A large staircase ran up the right-hand side of the space, taking a sharp left at a small landing and disappearing into the darkness above. Beside the staircase was a large table holding a porcelain bust and an arrangement of dried flowers. Left and right led off into small dark rooms, which appeared to lead deeper into the big house. Barnaby and Emily were waiting behind him.

'I think we should stick together. Barnaby – where do you think is the most likely place to find this entity?'

'Let's try the old wing first – it looks like the biggest space in the house from the outside. So,' he paused, 'I believe that means we take a left.'

They set off, heading towards the older part of the building, ducking their heads beneath the low doorways as they worked their way deeper into the building.

Emily hugged herself as they walked, feeling the chill. 'Do you think it knows we're here?'

Honoré caught her eye. 'It doesn't look like there's anyone else around. It depends on whether it knows what has happened to the two guards, or whether they were under its control.'

Barnaby coughed lightly into his hand. He was twitchy now, obviously nervous, but, Honoré could see, determined to complete his task. He could see now why the man had so desperately sought out their help, even across time – this was not a job for one man alone. If Barnaby truly was fading away – which Honoré believed he was – then he understood all too well the desire to make a last gasp, to finish what he had started and to make a difference with what time he had left. Honoré had seen that impulse many, many times during his years in the army.

The rooms in this part of the building were mostly interconnected, so the three of them passed through a number of smaller chambers before entering the old wing proper. Each of these rooms was largely devoid of artefacts or furniture; save for the odd table or a random chair, the left wing of the building seemed largely empty and uninhabited. Lechasseur supposed that whatever family did still live here inhabited only one small part of the whole building now.

Emily suddenly stopped walking and raised her hand in the air. The others stopped short to see what was wrong.

'Emily, are you ...' began Lechasseur.

'Shhh.' She cut him off. 'Can you hear that?'

Barnaby cocked his head in an exaggerated expression of compliance. 'Oh my goodness, yes I can.' He looked startled, strangely entranced. Honoré strained to hear too.

There was a hollow, tinkling sound coming from somewhere ahead of them. Honoré guessed it was a few rooms away, but it was certainly there. He listened more intently. It had a bizarre, abstract quality to it, an almost musical tone, as if someone were speaking – or singing. He couldn't detect any real melody or words, but nevertheless could feel himself being drawn into it, losing himself in its sweet complexity. He shook his head to try to clear it. He watched the other two for a moment. They were clearly caught up in the strange music too, taking in all its connotations, its details, its layers.

Honoré cleared his throat, trying to get their attention. 'Let's keep going. We're obviously heading in the right direction. Remember why we're here – don't get caught up in it all. Think of the people in the village who can't wake themselves out of the trance. We don't want to end up the same way.'

Barnaby shook his head, looking dazed. 'You're right, quite right. Let's concentrate and keep moving.' He stepped towards the closed door at the other side of the empty room, his footsteps echoing loudly on the wooden floor. Just as he was about to turn the handle, he hesitated, and looked back at Honoré and Emily, smiling.

'I just wanted to say thank you, before we go any further.' He nodded to them, as if he knew something of what was about to happen. 'Now watch yourselves in there.' He clicked open the door and stepped into the adjoining room.

The two travellers stood for a moment, as if waiting to see what would happen next. Then Emily grabbed hold of Lechasseur's arm and pulled him onwards, after the severed man.

The next chamber was similar to the last, devoid of all personality and life, except that the sound of the strange music was more distinct here, and there was a bright light seeping underneath an old, misshapen door in the far wall, giving Emily the impression that to open it would be to flood the room with an abyss of whiteness, of bright nothingness. It was as if the door was holding back a tide of some sort, and to open it would bring about the end of the world, drowning everyone in the strange glow, deafening them with the oddly symphonic sound. For a moment she wanted to do nothing else but scream and run from the house, as far away from Barnaby and his terrible time entity as possible, or else grab hold of Lechasseur and force him to time hop back to 1950 and the safety of home. But then she composed herself with a deep breath, glanced briefly at Honoré, and stepped forward, opening the door.

For a moment they were all blind.

Light seared Honoré's eyes, burning them to dry, hot stones that ached in the harsh, baking incandescence. He tried to cover his face with the crook of his arm, but to no avail. Beside him, he thought he could hear Emily screaming. The strange music had changed in tempo, picking up rhythm, increasing greatly in intensity. He felt as if his eardrums would burst at any moment.

Then the light changed shape.

It was the most bizarre thing that Lechasseur had ever witnessed. Suddenly there was a different *texture* to the light, and the pain in his eyes subsided. He wiped at his streaming face. It was as if the whole room had *shifted*, or something had altered, and now he could see again.

He blinked and looked around, still struggling to see against the intense brightness, but able now to make out more of what was going on. The music still rang loudly in his ears.

His first sight was the room itself. It was a great hall, a huge, expansive space, created by the void beneath the two felled trees, which still appeared to prop the building up, resting against each other as they had done for centuries, holding everything in place. There was no furniture anywhere to be seen.

The first thing that really struck him, however, inspiring a moment of stunned inaction, was the sight of a hundred or so people crowding around the edges of the room. They were all shuffling their feet like animated zombies, all entirely consumed by the bizarre music, all facing towards the light as if it were warming their faces, washing into their very souls. Their faces were images of rapture, or religious ecstasy, and Honoré was utterly appalled by the sight of it.

He looked up towards the source of the light itself.

The creature was both exquisitely beautiful and horrifyingly obscene. It hung amongst the rafters like some kind of archangel or hovering ghost. At first, Honoré could make out nothing but painful, shining light, but the more he looked, the more detail he saw.

The entity was almost gaseous in nature; an amorphous, globular body of shifting intensity, shining out from a central nucleus like a miniature sun or an atomic explosion. Yet *inside* the body of the alien thing were strange, interlocking, geometric shapes, patterns of differently textured light, drifting around, colliding with one another to form new patterns, new helix-like shapes and strands of what Lechasseur assumed to be signs of life, of intelligence. He watched for a moment, entirely caught up in the sight of it.

The dissonant, discordant sound continued to float around the room, captivating him. It was as if his mind had begun to fill in the blanks in the patterns, predicting what would happen next, filling in the spaces between sounds with the missing notes. It occurred to him how entirely clever it all was, how easily it had arrested his attention and drawn him in. The music played out all around him, a symphony of ecstasy.

He studied the shapes for a moment longer. He thought, for a moment, that he had caught the flicker of a face in the patterns, a disembodied human visage looking down at him, its mouth moving in a silent, imploring chant. He looked harder now, trying to search it out amongst the storm of chaos.

And then he caught sight of it again. Only it wasn't a human face at all, but something far, far worse. Something indescribable, skull-like, utterly terrifying. It screamed, and the whole world came crashing down around Honoré's ears.

He was back in the fields of Normandy, fishing for his rifle amongst a putrid pile of warm body parts, trying desperately to reclaim his only defence against the oncoming swarm of enemy soldiers. His hands were slick with blood, his eyes stinging with the smoke and the sweat and the sight of his lost companions.

He was standing on the riverbank back in London, struggling against Abraxas, the horrible man-thing with his rasping, ragged breath and his stench of old, worn leather and blood.

He was a small child in New Orleans, struggling desperately to save himself from drowning in the bayou, where his foot had become trapped in the reeds after a secret night-time swim. The water tasted foul on the back of his tongue as he lapped at the air, trying to stay afloat. His parents were asleep inside.

He was at his mother's bedside as she died of a wicked cancer, her entire chest eaten away by the growth, as if she were so much cattle feed, a thin bag of flesh and bones stretched out on the bed. He didn't want to kiss her, as her skin tasted of salt and stale urine.

He was dead, lying in a quiet grave, unmarked and heaped with cloying soil and dirt. He couldn't move, couldn't even turn his head to see the worms that were crawling beneath his skin, burrowing into his flesh as his body became one with the earth once again.

He was …

Lying on the floor in the great hall, Emily slapping his face hard with the palm of her hand, screaming his name at the top of her lungs.

'Honoré! Honoré! Wake up, damn you! Honoré!'

He looked at her with a start.

'What the …?'

'It's killing him. It's tearing him apart.' Emily sobbed and allowed herself to slip to the floor beside him. He scrambled to his feet. This time, his view of the entity was entirely different.

It was like trying to take in the view of a million years all at once. The time streams around him were wide open, whipping around like some complex shape devised by Escher, a universe of time and space. The time-snake of the entity was like a broiling, complex web, and

Barnaby was at the centre of it, thrashing against the flow like some tiny child trying to stop the revolution of the world. All around him, terrifying skeletal faces screamed at him, tormenting him with their aeons-worth of agony. And Barnaby continued to be consumed by the thing, to be dissolved by the sheer *weight* of its presence, the sheer pressure of time, to dissipate into nothing but a few broken strands of severed time.

But Honoré could see it now, could see the entity for what it truly was, and he knew he could do nothing to save Barnaby from his misdirected last gasp.

He reached out and grabbed hold of Emily, pulling her hard to her feet.

'Come on! We've got to get back to 1950. We have to stop him; we have to stop him killing it there! We need to go now, before it's too late. There's nothing more we can do here.' He spun her around, still sobbing, and together they traced the dissolving shape of the severed man from amongst the searing chaos and disappeared in a haze of blue electrical light.

PART FOUR: THE LIGHT OF OTHER DAYS

SEVERENCE

The darkness was a respite after the painful light; a blanket of calm, soothing away the shock of the last few minutes. Honoré slowly became aware of his surroundings.

It was raining, hard. The water lashed at him, stinging his upturned face. He looked around, stumbling momentarily with the disorientation.

1950. The graveyard.

The step through time had left him tired and drained. He rested his hand on a nearby tombstone and looked around for Emily in the dark storm. The wind was howling, driving the rain at him from a sharp, almost horizontal angle. Honoré could feel the water penetrating his clothes, soaking him through to the skin. He opened his mouth to call out for Emily, but the sound was carried away by the wind, and the rainwater flowed into his open mouth, causing him to hack and splutter. He could barely see a thing.

He pushed himself away from the old grave, trying to steady himself. He couldn't see Emily anywhere. He staggered over to a clump of nearby trees, realisation dawning on him that the grave he had been standing beside had been that of Barnaby Tewkes. He wondered whether it was empty or not.

Behind Lechasseur, the ruined church stood like an old monolith against the night sky, holding steady against the severe weather. He figured Emily might have tried to make it inside to find shelter. He clambered around the tree trunks, feeling his way so as not to fall. He staggered from gravestone to gravestone, catching hold of each one as he passed, to stop the wind from stealing his footing in the muddy loam. In the distance he could see the street lamps glowing with a dull electrical haze, washed out by the insistent rain.

He steadied himself. Just as he was about to try and make a run for the church entrance, he caught a glimpse of some dark blue fabric from around the back of one of the larger gravestones. He circled it, finding Emily slumped in a heap on the ground, her face muddied and her hair pressed into the dirt. She looked pale, cold and wet.

Lechasseur knelt down beside his companion and scooped her up in his arms, staggering under the extra weight. He felt his feet sinking into the mud. Emily was unconscious, and he needed to get her to safety as soon as possible. He made a concerted effort to jog towards the church doorway and ducked inside, bringing them out of the harsh conditions and into the relative shelter of the burnt-out building.

There was no door left on the old church, and a huge part of the ceiling had collapsed in on itself, so the building was still exposed to the elements, but Honoré managed to find a sheltered corner to place Emily down on the ground. He took his coat from around his shoulders and gently laid it over her, resting her head carefully on the flagged stone floor.

She looked like she had been attacked; she had a large red welt across her right cheek and it was clear she had been battered and pushed into the mud.

Lechasseur punched the side of his leg in frustration.

Someone had obviously been waiting for them when they arrived back in 1950, and had either attacked Emily whilst she was still disorientated or had been provoked by her into defending himself. There was no doubt in his mind who was responsible.

The severed man.

The crazed, bewildered incarnation of Barnaby Tewkes that inhabited this era.

He shook his head. Barnaby had got it all wrong.

When Lechasseur had seen the magnificent, twisting time-snake of the entity back in 1921, he had been afforded a singular insight into its bizarre, formless mind. It had seemed, at the time, like a hot needle lancing him between the eyes, burning into his brain; a series of elaborate, flickering images being forced into his mind's eye, playing out like a long sequence of film. It was almost as if the creature was trying to speak to him, to communicate through its pained expressions, forcing him to witness its own plight first-hand, to suffer its agonies and trade its memories for his own. He had been dragged painfully through his own timeline, forced to relive many of his own difficult experiences, even to witness what he thought was his own death, or at least his post-life, his decomposition. Yet the entity had given as much as it had taken, providing insights into its own existence, trying to make him *understand.*

It was dying, just like the severed man.

Honoré had witnessed a terrible glimpse of the future, had seen the entity tormented by nightmarish, ghostly figures. The figures had been slicing away at its time-snake like ethereal butchers, carving the alien creature into ribbons of pain. It had fled into human history in an attempt to hide, to flee its torment, but its enemies had pursued it and sought it out, bending it to their will.

It was a victim, not an accomplice; as persecuted as the bastardised remains of the soldier he had helped to die in the glowing flames of the cultists' godforsaken house.

He had to find the boy before Barnaby did. The boy was the key. The boy was the entity, its manifestation in this time period. If he could only try to *talk* to it again, to explain somehow the pain and hurt that its continued presence was inadvertently causing, the danger that it represented to all the other time sensitive people throughout history, Honoré was convinced he could make a difference.

But if Barnaby got to it first …

He looked down at Emily to see that she was stirring. He wiped her brow with the edge of his sleeve.

'Emily? Emily, are you okay?'

Her eyes flicked open with a start, and she tried to sit up, suddenly frantic. 'Where is he? What has he done?'

'You're okay, Emily, we're alone. What has who done?' He knew very well to whom she was referring.

'Barnaby.' She gasped for breath, her eyes flicking from side to side as if she expected him to reappear at any moment. 'He was waiting for us when we arrived. I tried to talk to him, to ask him if he was okay, if he remembered what had happened back in the village, but he just attacked me, went for me like some sort of monster, slashing away at me with his grubby hands. The last thing I remember is hitting the ground in the rain, banging my head on the gravestone. He must think we abandoned him to that horrible time creature in 1921.'

Honoré nodded. 'He's got it all wrong, Emily. Horribly wrong. The creature isn't trying to hurt anyone. It's *running away*, trying to hide from its own execution in the far future. It's just like him, like Barnaby. Someone – or something – is trying to kill it.'

'How do you …'

'I *saw* it. I saw its time-snake when Barnaby was trying to fight it. I think there must be some sort of connection between them, something that links their deaths.'

'The time-cult?' Emily was trying to sit up, her head aching and her body slick with wet and mud.

'Perhaps.'

'But what about the Devil cult? And the villagers? How do you explain them?'

Honoré helped her to her feet as he spoke, placing his coat around her shoulders. 'The Cabal were holding the creature prisoner, tormenting it and forcing it to make contact with the time sensitives in that era. They were using it as a compass, an unwilling navigator of the time streams, to help them locate their victims. It showed me all this as it tried to prevent Barnaby from obliterating himself.' He sighed. 'The villagers were something different again. I think it was trying to protect them, wrap them up inside a bubble of time and stop them from witnessing what was really going on. I guess it must have failed to keep them contained.' He shrugged. 'But we have to go after Barnaby and stop him. If he's found the boy, it may already be too late.'

Emily met his gaze. 'So you've worked out the connection to the boy, too?' She looked a little bewildered.

'The boy *is* the entity.'

'Oh no.'

'We have to go after them.'

'But the boy was there too, in the graveyard, watching in the rain.'

Honoré's expression changed. 'When Barnaby attacked you?'

She nodded. Honoré put a hand on Emily's shoulder. 'Wait here.' He charged out into the pouring rain.

Outside, the rain was cascading from the heavens, veiling everything in a watery mist. Honoré put his hand to his head, wishing that he hadn't lost his hat. He scanned the graveyard, trying to catch any sign of the crazed Barnaby or the child.

Nothing.

He staggered out into the full force of the storm, looking from side –to side, stopping every few feet to check behind him. Emily was standing in the doorway of the old church, shivering, his jacket pulled tightly around her small frame. It was then that he had the idea.

He ran towards the edge of the graveyard and scrambled over the wall, nearly slipping on the old, moss-covered stones. He dropped to his feet on the other side and, just glancing around to check he hadn't missed them in his haste, made his way down toward the marketplace.

One of the streetlamps was buzzing with electricity as he stood beneath it for a moment, waiting, hoping. The rain continued to hammer down on him, thrumming on the top of his head as he tried to catch his breath.

And then he heard it. The scuff of a heel from just around the corner. He looked up from sheltering his face. The boy was running across the marketplace, heading in the direction of the churchyard.

'Wait!' he called after the entity-child, hoping it would stop. It kept on running, its scarf flapping in the wind and the rain as it went.

Honoré took off after the boy, throwing himself along the street, his feet skidding dangerously on the wet cobbles, splashing in the shallow puddles and the streaming channels of water that ran along the roadside like miniature rivers.

He rounded the bend, not sure what he expected to see. He hoped it wasn't going to be Emily in her pink pyjamas ...

Barnaby was there, standing in the pounding rain, his long,

bedraggled hair loose down his back, his beard wet and shining. He looked like some sort of monster, laughing to himself, his hands wrapped around the throat of the child, attempting to squeeze the life out of it. The boy was flapping his hands, trying to wriggle free.

Honoré charged towards them, shouting as he ran. 'Barnaby! Leave him. It's not what you think.'

Barnaby's head flicked to one side to regard the charging man. He continued to laugh like some deranged hyena, his hands tightening their grip.

Lechasseur crashed headlong into the side of the other man, sending them both sprawling onto the pavement. Barnaby let out a harsh wheeze as the air was knocked from his lungs. They both lay there on the damp street for a moment, trying to regain their breath.

Honoré climbed to his feet. The other man was folded in half, clutching at his belly. Honoré nudged him with his foot, deciding that he was safe for a moment. He scanned around, looking for the entity-child.

The boy was standing a few yards away, watching him intently. Honoré hesitated. Last time he had tried to approach, the boy had taken flight, hurtling off down the street at a phenomenal pace. He took a short step forward towards the boy.

It continued to stare at him.

Lechasseur edged closer, trying not to spook the creature into running away. He didn't know if he had the energy left to chase after it again.

The boy opened its mouth, and the whole street was suddenly flooded in light. Honoré watched as the child's head simply folded back on itself, unwrapping the creature inside like the peeling of an banana skin or the shedding of a rubber sleeve. The light shone out against the darkness and the rain, seemingly burning away the tempestuous night.

Honoré marvelled at the entity once again. He could see the strange shapes swirling about inside it, and could hear, now, the bizarre tinkling music that he supposed was its voice. He allowed his eyes to focus, to unveil the spinning time streams that encased the alien thing, enabling him to look deeper into its history. None of it made any sense. It was entirely *other*. This was an entity so alien to him, so outside his experience, that he could hardly comprehend its existence. Yet he needed to find some way to communicate with it.

He closed his eyes, trying to visualise his thoughts, trying to give shape and form to the abstract concepts in his mind. The entity seemed to respond, alternating the patterns in its musical voice, pulsating as if it were trying to say something back. Lechasseur continued to try to broadcast his message.

Images began to flow through his mind once again, pushing everything else out of the way. It was like attempting to comprehend a whole universe of different spacial dimensions all at once. None of the images made any real sense. Occasionally, he would catch a glimpse of a human-like shape, or a shadowy figure in the background, but most of it slipped by him unchecked. The pain was all too real, however, and he felt as if his brain was burning inside his skull, roiling like a storm cloud about to heave its heavy load.

He forced himself to relax, and focused, drawing out the images of the murdered corpses, the devil worshippers, the enthralled village people, and the fractured remains of Barnaby Tewkes.

Something changed.

Honoré opened his eyes. The light was gone. He glanced around, trying to see in the dark, spots of light dancing in front of his vision where the intense light had been just a moment before.

The boy was gone too. There was no sign of the creature anywhere.

He didn't know what to make of it. Lechasseur glanced down at Barnaby, who was still lying on the ground by the side of the road, a sorry mess. He would have to think of something he could do to help the poor man. Perhaps he could get him admitted to some sort of asylum or care home. He rubbed at his eyes and turned about, only just realising that Emily had appeared behind him. She still had his coat wrapped around her shoulders, sheltering slightly from the heavy rain. She smiled. 'What happened?'

'I'm not sure, but I think it's going to be okay.' He shrugged. 'I guess time will tell. The entity seems to have gone, for now. But we've other things to deal with. All that business with the Devil. We'll have to sort that out, too.' He bowed his head slightly, trying to catch her eye. He looked tired.

'But not now ... HONORÉ!' She screamed as she grabbed hold of him, trying to spin him around. He almost fell to the ground as he turned to see Barnaby launching himself towards them, a wicked grin on his face, his hands outstretched as if he planned to rake at them with his ragged nails.

Honoré staggered backwards, Emily clutching onto him, trying not to fall.

There was a flash of blue light, and suddenly they were gone.

THE TOWER

The landscape was desolate, a metropolis of concrete and glass. Honoré scanned the horizon. He had no idea what had happened. Emily was standing beside him.

'What was that?' he asked.

'We time jumped.'

'But how?' He was still dripping with rainwater, rivulets of it running down his face, stinging his eyes. He wiped ineffectually at his face.

'I have no idea. But it must have had something to do with Barnaby.' She looked at him and shrugged. 'Any idea where the hell we are?'

'No. But I don't like the look of that at all.' He nodded toward the large tower block in front of them, an immense shard of glass and metal that stabbed at the night sky like it was trying to puncture the underside of the clouds.

'Well, we can't stand here in these wet clothes. Let's go and check it out. We need to find somewhere to rest, so we can try to make sense of what's been going on, and figure out where the hell we are.'

'Okay, let's go.'

As they walked, they realised it was snowing gently. Their feet crunched through the white powder, and both tugged their clothes around them as they started to shiver.

The two travellers, walking closely side-by-side, slowly approached the large building, both of them tired and nervous after all that had gone on, both of them unsure how they were even going to start the process of unravelling and making sense of all of the events that had occurred over the last few days.

As Honoré had said, Emily mused, only time would tell.

In the meantime, the tower waited for them like a dark obelisk, a bleak temptation of the future.

THE STORY CONTINUES IN *TIME HUNTER: ECHOES*

ABOUT THE AUTHOR

George Mann was born in Darlington, County Durham, in 1978. He has been reading science fiction since he first managed to lay his hands on a copy of *The War of the Worlds* on his eleventh birthday.

He is the former editor of *Outland* magazine, writes an SF column for the internet and is the author of *The Mammoth Encyclopaedia of Science Fiction*. He is currently putting the finishing touches to a new work of SF criticism.

The Human Abstract for Telos Publishing was his first work of fiction, and *The Severed Man* is his second.

He lives in Tamworth, Staffordshire, with his wife, son and encroaching library, and when not writing, works as an international books consultant for a gaming company.

ACKNOWLEDGEMENTS

With thanks as ever to Fiona and James, to the Sales & Marketing teams at BL, to Simon and Kate, to Mark Newton, to Daniel O'Mahony and all the Time Hunter writers, and to David, Rosemary and Steve for their faith in the books.

TIME HUNTER

A range of high-quality, original paperback and limited edition hardback novellas featuring the adventures in time of Honoré Lechasseur. Part mystery, part detective story, part dark fantasy, part science fiction ... these books are guaranteed to enthral fans of good fiction everywhere, and are in the spirit of our acclaimed range of *Doctor Who* Novellas.

ALREADY AVAILABLE

THE WINNING SIDE by LANCE PARKIN

Emily is dead! Killed by an unknown assailant. Honoré and Emily find themselves caught up in a plot reaching from the future to their past, and with their very existence, not to mention the future of the entire world, at stake, can they unravel the mystery before it is too late?

An adventure in time and space.

£7.99 (+ £1.50 UK p&p) Standard p/b ISBN 1-903889-35-9 (pb)

£25.00 (+ £1.50 UK p&p) Deluxe h/b ISBN 1-903889-36-7 (hb)

THE TUNNEL AT THE END OF THE LIGHT by STEFAN PETRUCHA

In the heart of post-war London, a bomb is discovered lodged at a disused station between Green Park and Hyde Park Corner. The bomb detonates, and as the dust clears, it becomes apparent that *something* has been awakened. Strange half-human creatures attack the workers at the site, hungrily searching for anything containing sugar ...

Meanwhile, Honoré and Emily are contacted by eccentric poet Randolph Crest, who believes himself to be the target of these subterranean creatures. The ensuing investigation brings Honoré and Emily up against a terrifying force from deep beneath the earth, and one which even with their combined powers, they may have trouble stopping.

An adventure in time and space.

£7.99 (+ £1.50 UK p&p) Standard p/b ISBN 1-903889-37-5 (pb)

£25.00 (+ £1.50 UK p&p) Deluxe h/b ISBN 1-903889-38-3 (hb)

THE CLOCKWORK WOMAN by CLAIRE BOTT

Honoré and Emily find themselves imprisoned in the 19th Century by a celebrated inventor … but help comes from an unexpected source – a humanoid automaton created by and to give pleasure to its owner. As the trio escape to London, they are unprepared for what awaits them, and at every turn it seems impossible to avert what fate may have in store for the Clockwork Woman.

An adventure in time and space.

£7.99 (+ £1.50 UK p&p) Standard p/b ISBN 1-903889-39-1 (pb)
£25.00 (+ £1.50 UK p&p) Deluxe h/b ISBN 1-903889-40-5 (hb)

KITSUNE by JOHN PAUL CATTON

In the year 2020, Honoré and Emily find themselves thrown into a mystery, as an ice spirit – *Yuki-Onna* – wreaks havoc during the Kyoto Festival, and a haunted funhouse proves to contain more than just paper lanterns and wax dummies. But what does all this have to do with the elegant owner of the Hide and Chic fashion chain … and to the legendary Chinese fox-spirits, the Kitsune?

An adventure in time and space.

£7.99 (+ £1.50 UK p&p) Standard p/b ISBN 1-903889-41-3 (pb)
£25.00 (+ £1.50 UK p&p) Deluxe h/b ISBN 1-903889-42-1 (hb)

COMING SOON

ECHOES by IAIN MCLAUGHLIN & CLAIRE BARTLETT

Echoes of the past … echoes of the future. Honoré Lechasseur can see the threads that bind the two together, however when he and Emily Blandish find themselves outside the imposing tower-block headquarters of Dragon Industry, both can sense something is wrong. There are ghosts in the building, and images and echoes of all times pervade the structure. But what is behind this massive contradiction in time, and can Honoré and Emily figure it out before they become trapped themselves …?

An adventure in time and space.

£7.99 (+ £1.50 UK p&p) Standard p/b ISBN 1-903889-45-6 (pb)
£25.00 (+ £1.50 UK p&p) Deluxe h/b ISBN 1-903889-46-4 (hb)
PUB: MARCH 2005 (UK)

TIME HUNTER FILM

DAEMOS RISING by DAVID J HOWE, DIRECTED BY KEITH BARNFATHER

Daemos Rising is a sequel to both the *Doctor Who* adventure *The Daemons* and to *Downtime*, an earlier drama featuring the Yeti. It is also a prequel of sorts to Telos Publishing's *Time Hunter* series. It stars Miles Richardson as ex-UNIT operative Douglas Cavendish, and Beverley Cressman as Brigadier Lethbridge-Stewart's daughter Kate. Trapped in an isolated cottage, Cavendish thinks he is seeing ghosts. The only person who might understand and help is Kate Lethbridge-Stewart ... but when she arrives, she realises that Cavendish is key in a plot to summon the Daemons back to the Earth. With time running out, Kate discovers that sometimes even the familiar can turn out to be your worst nightmare. Also starring Andrew Wisher, and featuring Ian Richardson as the Narrator.
An adventure in time and space.
£14.00 (+ £2.50 UK p&p) PAL format R4 DVD
Order direct from Reeltime Pictures, PO Box 23435, London SE26 5WU

HORROR/FANTASY

CAPE WRATH by PAUL FINCH
Death and horror on a deserted Scottish island as an ancient Viking warrior chief returns to life.
£8.00 (+ £1.50 UK p&p) Standard p/b ISBN: 1-903889-60-X

KING OF ALL THE DEAD by STEVE LOCKLEY & PAUL LEWIS
The king of all the dead will have what is his.
£8.00 (+ £1.50 UK p&p) Standard p/b ISBN: 1-903889-61-8

GUARDIAN ANGEL by STEPHANIE BEDWELL-GRIME
Devilish fun as Guardian Angel Porsche Winter loses a soul to the devil …
£9.99 (+ £2.50 UK p&p) Standard p/b ISBN: 1-903889-62-6

FALLEN ANGEL by STEPHANIE BEDWELL-GRIME
Porsche Winter battles she devils on Earth …
£9.99 (+ £2.50 UK p&p) Standard p/b ISBN: 1-903889-69-3

ASPECTS OF A PSYCHOPATH by ALISTAIR LANGSTON
Goes deeper than ever before into the twisted psyche of a serial killer. Horrific, graphic and gripping, this book is not for the squeamish.
£8.00 (+ £1.50 UK p&p) Standard p/b ISBN: 1-903889-63-4

SPECTRE by STEPHEN LAWS
The inseparable Byker Chapter: six boys, one girl, growing up together in the back streets of Newcastle. Now memories are all that Richard Eden has left, and one treasured photograph. But suddenly, inexplicably, the images of his companions start to fade, and as they vanish, so his friends are found dead and mutilated. Something is stalking the Chapter, picking them off one by one, something connected with their past, and with the girl they used to know.
£9.99 (+ £2.50 UK p&p) Standard p/b ISBN: 1-903889-72-3

THE HUMAN ABSTRACT by GEORGE MANN
A future tale of private detectives, AIs, Nanobots, love and death.
£7.99 (+ £1.50 UK p&p) Standard p/b ISBN: 1-903889-65-0

BREATHE by CHRISTOPHER FOWLER
The Office meets *Night of the Living Dead.*
£7.99 (+ £1.50 UK p&p) Standard p/b ISBN: 1-903889-67-7
£25.00 (+ £1.50 UK p&p) Deluxe h/b ISBN: 1-903889-68-5

HOUDINI'S LAST ILLUSION by STEVE SAVILE
Can the master illusionist Harry Houdini outwit the dead shades of his past?
£7.99 (+ £1.50 UK p&p) Standard p/b ISBN: 1-903889-66-9

ALICE'S JOURNEY BEYOND THE MOON by R J CARTER
A sequel to the classic Lewis Carroll tales.
£6.99 (+ £1.50 UK p&p) Standard p/b ISBN: 1-903889-76-6
£30.00 (+ £1.50 UK p&p) Deluxe h/b ISBN: 1-903889-77-4

TV/FILM GUIDES

A DAY IN THE LIFE: THE UNOFFICIAL AND UNAUTHORISED GUIDE TO 24 by KEITH TOPPING

Complete episode guide to the first season of the popular TV show.
£9.99 (+ £2.50 p&p) Standard p/b ISBN: 1-903889-53-7

THE TELEVISION COMPANION: THE UNOFFICIAL AND UNAUTHORISED GUIDE TO DOCTOR WHO by DAVID J HOWE & STEPHEN JAMES WALKER

Complete episode guide to the popular TV show.
£14.99 (+ £4.75 UK p&p) Standard p/b ISBN: 1-903889-51-0

LIBERATION: THE UNOFFICIAL AND UNAUTHORISED GUIDE TO BLAKE'S 7 by ALAN STEVENS & FIONA MOORE

Complete episode guide to the popular TV show.
Featuring a foreword by David Maloney
£9.99 (+ £2.50 UK p&p) Standard p/b ISBN: 1-903889-54-5

HOWE'S TRANSCENDENTAL TOYBOX: SECOND EDITION by DAVID J HOWE & ARNOLD T BLUMBERG

Complete guide to *Doctor Who* Merchandise.
£25.00 (+ £4.75 UK p&p) Standard p/b ISBN: 1-903889-56-1

HOWE'S TRANSCENDENTAL TOYBOX: 2003 EDITION by DAVID J HOWE & ARNOLD T BLUMBERG

Complete guide to *Doctor Who* Merchandise released in 2003.
£7.99 (+ £1.50 UK p&p) Standard p/b ISBN: 1-903889-57-X

A VAULT OF HORROR by KEITH TOPPING

A Guide to 80 Classic (and not so classic) British Horror Films
£12.99 (+ £4.75 UK p&p) Standard p/b ISBN: 1-903889-58-8

HANK JANSON

Classic pulp crime thrillers from the 1940s and 1950s.

TORMENT by HANK JANSON
£9.99 (+ £1.50 UK p&p) Standard p/b ISBN: 1-903889-80-4

WOMEN HATE TILL DEATH by HANK JANSON
£9.99 (+ £1.50 UK p&p) Standard p/b ISBN: 1-903889-81-2

SOME LOOK BETTER DEAD by HANK JANSON
£9.99 (+ £1.50 UK p&p) Standard p/b ISBN: 1-903889-82-0

SKIRTS BRING ME SORROW by HANK JANSON
£9.99 (+ £1.50 UK p&p) Standard p/b ISBN: 1-903889-83-9

WHEN DAMES GET TOUGH by HANK JANSON
£9.99 (+ £1.50 UK p&p) Standard p/b ISBN: 1-903889-85-5

ACCUSED by HANK JANSON
£9.99 (+ £1.50 UK p&p) Standard p/b ISBN: 1-903889-86-3

KILLER by HANK JANSON
£9.99 (+ £1.50 UK p&p) Standard p/b ISBN: 1-903889-87-1

FRAILS CAN BE SO TOUGH by HANK JANSON
£9.99 (+ £1.50 UK p&p) Standard p/b ISBN: 1-903889-88-X

THE TRIALS OF HANK JANSON by STEVE HOLLAND
£12.99 (+ £2.50 UK p&p) Standard p/b ISBN: 1-903889-84-7

The prices shown are correct at time of going to press. However, the publishers reserve the right to increase prices from those previously advertised without prior notice.

TELOS PUBLISHING
c/o Beech House, Chapel Lane, Moulton, Cheshire, CW9 8PQ, England
Email: orders@telos.co.uk
Web: www.telos.co.uk

To order copies of any Telos books, please visit our website where there are full details of all titles and facilities for worldwide credit card online ordering, or send a cheque or postal order (UK only) for the appropriate amount (including postage and packing), together with details of the book(s) you require, plus your name and address to the above address. Overseas readers please send two international reply coupons for details of prices and postage rates.